Christmas in Evergreen

Christmas in Evergreen

Heart of Evergreen

Book 1

By

Mary L. Schmidt

Christmas In Evergreen
Mary L. Schmidt

Copyright © 2023
by Mary Schmidt (M. Schmidt Productions)

Book and cover painting and design by Mary L. Schmidt

BISAC Subject Headings:
Fiction / Christian / Romance / Suspense
Fiction / Crime
Fiction / Thrillers / Psychological

Library of Congress

ISBN- 979-8-218-28923-2 Paperback
ISBN-13: 979-8-218-28924-9

Ebook

CHRYSLER, DODGE, JEEP®, RAM, MOPAR®, SRT copyright
FCA US LLC (FCA)

First edition published December 31, 2023

Blog (https://www.whenangelsfly.net)
Facebook (https://www.facebook.com/MMSchmidtAuthorGDDonley)
Twitter (https://twitter.com/MaryLSchmidt)
Deviant Art (http://mschmidtartwork.deviantart.com/)

Table of Contents

Dedication

Always to Shane, and Sammy, who taught us so much about life, bravery, and that a baby and a five-year-old can be wiser beyond their brief time on Earth,

Always to Gene, our son, who we cherish so much, and has been wise beyond his years, and has turned into a kind man,

Always to Michael, my beloved husband, partner, and best friend in the entire world,

Always to Mary, my beloved wife, partner, and best friend in the entire world.

Prologue

"My husband, Steve, and I have always had a great relationship, married, for the last five years. He's a private investigator, and I have my artwork. Much of his work involved using a special laptop, one that was rugged and lockable, in his home office and I had my art studio where I could lose myself in painting and creativity. Life was wonderful, until the day I read a completely chilling and startling "Hit List" on his computer screen. Confusion ran supreme in my brain and then it hit me. My name was at the top of that list! Wait! What? No! Never! Yet I read "Kim Daily" plain as day. What would you do if you found out you were the next target on your husband's hit list? Steve intentionally left his laptop open for me to read. He simply can't be an assassin! I would know. Or would I? No! That's impossible! Steve has been the kindest husband for five years and he was a crack ass private investigator; not an assassin. Yet why was my name at the top of his hit list? Why did he even have a hit list? My mind reeling in shock, I had to do something to stay alive!"

PART I

Chapter One

Steve and I have always had a great relationship, with three years of dating before marriage in our church, Saint Joseph *Catholic Church*. We married when I was 20 and Steve was 25.

I wore a lovely, yet simple white tiered silk wedding gown with a heart shaped bodice and puffed sleeves. Chantilly lace overlaid my gown, and Steve was handsome in his dark grey tuxedo. Our wedding bands of yellow gold and round brilliant diamonds matched, and my engagement ring was a designer princess cut yellow diamond surrounded by round white brilliants in yellow gold. We've been married for five years, and we dated three years before marriage.

Steve's best man was Gary Moore, a man he worked with and our next-door neighbors. His wife, Nancy, had short brunette hair that contrasted with her mauve matron of honor dress. She was my best friend in Boston.

Steve had no living family, due to a tragic house fire, thus no one came to our wedding from his side of the family. My parents were killed in a motor vehicle accident shortly after our wedding. Dad was a careful driver, and to this day, I wonder how their car rolled down a steep ravine and caught on fire when the weather was nice, the road clear, and no skid marks. Police investigations came up with no clear reason. *In looking back, I realized that my parents were taken out, as a hit man would do, purely assassinated, but let me back up a bit...*

Much of Steve's work involved using a special laptop, one that was rugged and lockable, in his home office and he was rarely gone overnight, usually home for dinner, and always impeccably dressed to the nines. His six-foot, three-inch height was topped off with black hair, neatly trimmed, rather short with slight curls, and his chiseled face was perfect, dark shadow or clean shaved, with irresistible penetrating black eyes. Not one ounce of fat on him as he worked out in our home gym every day. He always garnered looks from other women, and some men, too.

On the other hand, I was rather short at five feet, three inches, trim, with seafoam green eyes, and my curly blonde hair cascaded down my back, unless I had it up and in a messy bun. I usually wore dark blue skinny jeans or leggings with black leather slides or boots of the same supple leather, and paired those with a lightweight shirt, usually silk, 100 percent cotton, linen, or a mixture of pieces. My *Nike* running shoes made my early morning runs a breeze even though I had back pain from untreated scoliosis as a child, and my back pain was getting worse.

My green eyes contrasted deeply with Steve's dark black and fathomless eyes - eyes I would lose myself in. I loved his eyes as I investigated their depths, I never grew tired of that, and he was wonderful and looked at me like I was his world, the only thing that mattered in his life. *Yet life can change in the blink of an eye.*

Now my husband worked various hours, understandably, but he was rarely away from home overnight. If Steve was away at night, he always called and talked to me and let me know that he was okay. Steve never spoke of his current investigations or his situations because I didn't need to know any of that, and his thought was if I didn't know, then no one would come after me, *"and that was his mantra…"*

I wasn't interested in his laptop because I didn't feel the need to know who his clients were, and it wasn't something that I was curious about. Steve always kept his laptop locked when not in use, and of course he had client information that he kept secret. He never deviated in this pattern, ever! *Until…*

My home art studio was the place I felt most comfortable, and I would lose myself in painting and creativity, in both oils, and watercolor, and digital graphic design. When painting or creating, my hair was up in a messy bun, and I wore a smock. I preferred painting in oil as oil is a much more forgiving medium. Not only did I paint in oil and watercolor, but the creative side of me loved working on digital art in my computer. I was surrounded by plants and great lighting from the windows which were dressed in cream lace drapes.

Most completed art pieces were taken down to my art gallery not far from our home, and it was open two days a week, Thursday, and Friday, from 10am to 3pm, and by appointment otherwise. Nancy worked at my gallery when opened, and we became great friends. Life was fine. *Or so I thought. Never in a million years would I've imagined the next day's events.*

Once a year, close to Christmas, Steve and I entertained and hosted a gallery showing with other artists' pieces on show. Both Gary and Nancy leant a hand at our major shows. Red and white wine flowed freely with the hors d'oeuvres, both cold and hot on display, artfully arranged on charcuterie boards. Most of the food was gone by the end of the evening, and by the time the events ended, most gallery pieces had been sold. Art was my world at home and at the gallery, and Steve was supportive.

Life was good in our Beacon Hill suburb of Boston. Our home was designed with river rock and wood, an older home such as most in Beacon Hill. Our circle drive brought cars up to the double dark brown heavy oak front doors that opened out to a wraparound porch with five stone steps leading up to it.

We renovated our home with new fixtures and fittings, and I decorated it. The basement was partly Steve's "man cave with a home gym" and the rest remained as our home theater and to entertain neighbors as they were basically the only couples we mixed with, other than those in the art world, and that was always at my gallery.

Recliners made of buttery soft dark brown leather with matching sofas and tables of varnished cherry wood, were scattered over our cream-colored carpeting in our home theater. The 90-inch *Samsung* television was front and center, surrounded by a stereo system and our stone fireplace kept us cozy.

We spent much of our free time together in our basement. One full bath was in the corner, and I decorated it in cream and muted shades of rose. Our lighting was usually dimmed, and the wine rack was near the dark oak bar where we had various bottles of liquor and crystal glassware, in front of a long mirror behind the bar, and a built-in dishwasher. Five dark brown, soft leather bar stools sat in front, and we had a dark black refrigerator with an ice maker, so that was handy for snacks and colas.

From the foyer, one could see our first-floor open living space with a large living room, a stone fireplace, and we used it to entertain others or just ourselves. A double, curved, mahogany stairway graced the back of the foyer. Cream colored walls showed off my artworks.

Not only did we have another large television, but music flowed from the touch of a wall button. Above us hung a wonderful *Tiffany* chandelier - five tiers of gold-plated metal and crystal, with extra *Swarovski Crystals* that illuminated the room with adjustable lighting control. Matching lamps were designed like the chandelier above, and the room was large and cozy at the same time. Lighting could be muted at the touch of a button.

I had chosen to use reclaimed dark oak flooring that complemented the cream-colored walls mixed with dark mahogany paneling, and five of my paintings hung on the walls, most of them landscapes. I decorated it with comfortable black, buttery soft leather chairs and three sofas of the same black, buttery soft leather with gleaming, dark mahogany coffee and side tables.

Area rugs were scattered around, and one wall was a rich mahogany bookcase, full of treasured books, and some sculptures that I labored over to make perfect for us. This was our room for entertaining neighbors and included a wet bar made of – you got it – mahogany wood that gleamed with polish just like the rest of the wood pieces in the room. Our housekeeper, Susan, was worth her weight in gold as she made sure dust was gone and the wood gleamed.

Susan was 50, a widow, slim with gorgeous dark hair peppered with gray. She had a first-floor bedroom with an ensuite for herself, and we adored her. Susan was wonderful and the heavy cleaning and floor polishing was hired out routinely, when needed. She had full use of our first floor except for Steve's office and my studio, and she did our laundry or sent clothes to the dry cleaners who delivered them back to us.

Susan had become family to us both, and she was able to come and go, for groceries or to see her grandchildren, when she took time off. Susan's working relationship with us was extremely flexible, and we always gave her time off when family needs came up. In fact, I felt like she had become a second mother to me as we were that close!

Susan did our grocery shopping, fresh fruit and vegetables from the market, and our freezers were full of beef and pork. Steve and I enjoyed cooking our meals together, and Susan helped if we were entertaining. Steve always chose wine for our meals, as he was such a connoisseur, and we always shared our meals with Susan.

The rest of the first floor was comprised of Steve's office, my art studio, two full baths, a dining room with another *Tiffany* chandelier like the living room. The mahogany dining table and chairs seated up to 12 people, and I used antique mahogany side boards to match our table. Candles of different sizes graced the dining table and furniture. Rarely, if ever, did we have a full table, and only when neighbors were invited to come and celebrate an event, birthday, or holiday.

Through an arched open doorway, was our kitchen. I kept the mahogany tones with the cupboards, and we had a large black glass, double refrigerator, and appliances. Our kitchen was truly a chef's kitchen and we loved it. White marble countertops and a white marble topped island graced our kitchen. The white marble was exactly like the marble used on the Lincoln Memorial. We had the marble special ordered for our kitchen, and it came from Marble, Colorado, the only place it could be found. It was not unusual for any of us to take a break near the triple bay windows for breakfast or just for a cup of coffee or tea.

Down the hall was a marble and porcelain guest bathroom decorated in cream and peach tones, and further down from that was our laundry and mud room.

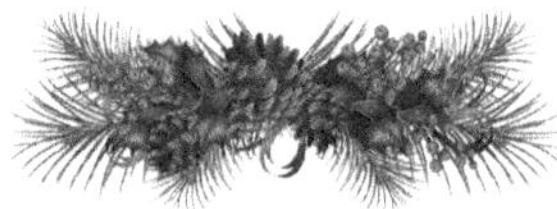

We had completely remodeled the second floor into one huge master ensuite with double sinks, hot tub, open double shower, and ornate oak wood graced the walls. We used blackout curtains and my closet, shoes, and jewelry collection rivaled anything the Kardashian's had - my walk-in closet went for miles, okay, not really, but I felt like it did.

I had a safe in my closet for jewelry and valuables. My closet was tidy with garments hanging up on racks, and I had shelves for shoes and heels and anything you could think of. Money was never an issue for us, and we lived life to the fullest. *Or so I thought we did…*

Steve had his own separate walk-in closet about half the size of mine. Suits from Armani and other high street clothiers hung next to each other from left to right starting with black and working down to a medium blue. Each shade sported several designer suits, and one side contained shirts in most colors and his silk tie collection - arranged by color from black to white.

A nice selection of shoes, leather dress shoes, hiking boots, and tennis shoes had the perfect spot. Steve had a built-in safe of his own in which he kept expensive watches, guns, and other items I had no idea of, stored inside, as I rarely ventured into his closet, and never into his safe. *I never knew the combination as it was a secret, or so Steve told me, so that I would be protected in case of a break in…*

Steve came to my closet though, and he offered his thoughts on my evening gowns and shoes. My intimate apparel fascinated him so much that he asked me to model different pieces like a fashion show about once a month, and I was happy to oblige.

Steve especially liked to see me in thong silk panties, barely-there, lace corsets or half cup bras, and sheer see-through, body-hugging material such as soft silk chiffon, and he truly loved those pieces that matched my skin tone and gave the illusion of nothing hiding my body from him.

He also loved my stilettos when I matched them to my lingerie. Steve was purely an ass man, although he would brag (to me) about how my nipples would harden with one look from his eyes.

We always ended up in our huge double king bed that dominated our bedroom. Our sex life was fantastic, our bodies fit together perfect, and even if we weren't making love, we slept and cuddled together in a perfect spooning state. I felt protected and safe in his arms.

Steve always told me, "I love you" and he left me little post it types of notes hidden in secret places where I would find them during my morning routine. I could be putting on my makeup and reach for a tube of lipstick, and there would be a small post-it notes with "I love you" written on it. Those notes meant more to me than all the diamonds, emeralds, rubies, sapphires, and pearls that he bought me.

We were fortunate to have a large backyard with perfect landscaping – yes – you guessed it – we had a caretaker/landscaper living in a small house with an attached garage in our huge backyard. Tom was 53, and he looked 45 with just a touch of gray at his temples. I think Tom quite liked Susan as I often caught them talking together, and she would make treats for Tom, on occasion, or invite him in for lunch.

Attached to our home was a three-car garage where we parked Steve's *Land Rover* and my *Jeep Grand Cherokee Limited*. Snow, or any kind of weather, wasn't a problem for us, and we loved making fresh tracks in the snow and going out on mountain trails any time of the year. Susan parked her *Subaru* in the third space.

Steve was ginormous on safety! We had a high-tech security system and codes were changed regularly. I had thought this was done out of love. *Yet now I have doubts…*

Steve's world was such that he wore a 9 mm *Ruger* on his person, in a side holster, when he was not at home, and when home, his *Ruger* was front and center on his desk. I knew detectives carried weapons, but Steve was a private investigator. I never questioned the need to carry a weapon, as Gary, next door, also wore one since he did the same type of investigative work.

Steve was adamant that I learned how to shoot weapons, and he bought me a black-on-black 22-gauge automatic *Ruger* of my own, and an automated 22-gauge revolver. Once a month we did target practice at our local shooting range. Steve was a dead on shot every single time, whereas I became good in that I did hit the target each time, but not a bull's eye like he was, and his style impressed me.

We both had concealed carry permits, I rarely took my *Ruger* with me when out in the suburbs in which we lived, and Steve would shake his head at me when I would go for a run without one of my guns.

We lived in a safe area, yet Steve felt that protection was required all the time. His rationale was for my safety, and I didn't understand why that was so in our neighborhood. So, I carried a gun part of the time, to make my husband happy for my safety.

As a private investigator, Steve did make enemies through his line of work, and he always cautioned me that there was a chance of someone trying to get back at him, and that would be through me, yet living in a gated and secure home, I didn't carry my gun with me from room to room. If someone got through our outer security, and they touched a window, alarms rang out loudly.

Essentially, if someone wanted to get back at Steve, and through me, that meant it would happen outside of our home. They would have to catch me between trips to my art gallery, and when I was at the gallery, of course.

I was open to business, and never really worried about it, because I didn't think Steve was overly concerned. Security cameras were placed both inside and outside. One push of a button on my smart watch would get the police to me fast.

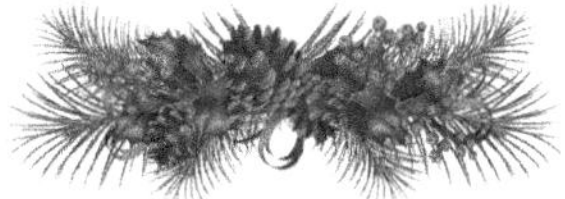

Last evening, we hosted Gary and Nancy, our next-door neighbors, for a lovely stir fry dinner with salad. Gary stood six feet tall with blonde hair and blue eyes on his athletic frame, and Nancy had fbrunette pixie hair and blue eyes on her slender yet tall frame.

Gary occasionally assisted Steve with cases and vice versa. I had heard them talking together when I walked into Steve's office to tell them dinner was ready. Both men glanced at each other rather oddly, and then followed me out the door and to the table.

The atmosphere was strained while eating, and I had no idea what was wrong or why both men spoke very little. *Did I overhear something I should not have? I only heard voices, not distinct words...*

Nancy was her usual talkative self, and she kept the conversation going with thoughts on possibly having a baby, and decorating a nursery in colors that would work for a baby boy or baby girl. We both talked of starting a family but neither man commented on our discussion.

As Nancy's excitement grew, so did mine. I was ready to start a family, but was Steve ready? He was not enthusiastic about our conversation. Steve was quiet throughout and when our meal was finished, Gary spoke up fast and stated that they had to get home and discuss the baby situation, rather than having the usual glass or two of wine. *How odd that was…but I didn't question it…*

Later, at bedtime, Steve gave me a quick kiss and stated he was worn out and needed rest. That was fine with me as rest is first, and we could talk about having a baby when he wasn't so tired. *Yet sinister things come out when least expected! Little did I know what was going to befall me…never in a million years…and so outrageously wrong and pure evil!*

Chapter Two

"What would you do if you found out you were the next target on your husband's hit list! Steve intentionally left his laptop open for me to read. He simply can't be an assassin! I would know. Or would I? No! That's impossible! Steve has been the kindest husband for five years and he was a crack ass private investigator; not an assassin. Yet why was my name at the top of his hit list? Why did he even have a hit list? My mind reeling in shock, I had to do something to stay alive! Think, Kim, think! Get your best game on now as time is running out!"

*T*oday started off like most mornings, when Susan was on holiday, we cooked breakfast together. Steve looked dapper in his dark blue, double breasted, two button Armani suit, light blue shirt, and dark blue striped silk tie! All the way down to his black socks and black leather boots with tread on them. Those grooves enabled him to run in all types of weather, if he was chasing a person he was investigating.

I always thought it was funny that Steve dressed to the nines yet imagining him running after someone in a designer suit was funny. I compared him to a *James Bond* type of hero. *Steve was my personal James Bond-ish hero-husband.*

As Steve headed out the door, I noticed his laptop was on and not locked. After giving me a quick kiss, I asked, "Do you want me to turn off your laptop for you?"

"That's not necessary, Kim," replied Steve with a wave of his hand. "I won't be gone long, maybe an hour or so. Truly it's no problem, but if you'd feel better, then do close it, please and thanks." Steve's look chilled me, icy cold and calculated, not his normal self. After giving Steve a tight smile and brief wave of my hand, I closed the door.

Naturally, I went in to close the laptop and I noticed a list of names on a document. As I was closing it, I caught a glimpse of my name. *How odd.* I looked closer at what Steve had been working on.

I couldn't believe what I saw on the screen. It was a hit list! Steve had a separate life I knew nothing about! How could he be an assassin? No way. No. Never in a million years would I ever have thought that Steve would be an assassin, and as I read more, it was clear that the list also contained names crossed out in red highlight – those already killed!

He kept records of all the people that he had assassinated, and I thought I would faint because it was too much to take in. Yet, why was my name at the top of his hit list? Why did he even have a hit list? What chilled me the most wasn't even the number of people he had assassinated (I didn't count them); it was my name on his list! Unbelievable! *Okay, Kim, make sure you read this correctly…Take a good look but be ready to run and hide!*

As chills washed over and through my body, I knew this was real life. Trembling, my mind raced. What do I do? With my brain reeling in shock, I had to do something to stay alive! Think, Kim, think! Get your best game on now as time is running out!

Steve would be back in less than one hour. Then it hit me, Steve had wanted me to see this list and my name! Was this some kind of cruel game he had played or was it for real? Could this be a cat and mouse fun game, ending up with sex upstairs, or not?

With little time to spare, I ran down the hall and up the stairs. Grabbing a tote bag, I shoved jeans, shirts, and essentials inside. Since I had my hiking boots on, I was good there. I shoved both my guns, extra clips, and ammunition inside my purse along with my mobile phone. But could I kill my husband if it came down to it? Yes, I had to run, and run fast! *The cold and chilling look in his black eyes told me to run, and I shivered at the memory of that look Steve gave to me a few minutes ago...who was this man I married?*

My mind raced as I shoved four bottles of water in with my gear and ran out to my Jeep, not bothering to lock the house's front door! I had to leave and hide. I had to protect myself. Boston was no longer safe for me, and Steve could return at any time! I had to play this out as a real event, simply because it could be real.

My Jeep started and I backed out and left not knowing where to go or what to do next. Steve could track me down, and I was grateful that I had filled the fuel tank yesterday. As I drove down the street, I tossed my cellphone out the window and into a ravine. I felt better that I could prevent being found due to my cellphone. *Think, Kim, think! How could I be traced?*

I realized I couldn't use my bank or credit cards as Steve would track me, so I went inside our bank and obtained five hundred thousand in cash, before dumping all my bank and credit cards in the trash. Then I went inside a discount store and purchased three burner phones. So far so good, but I was a nervous wreck!

Wracking my brain, I contemplated my next step. I knew Steve could easily find me in my Jeep, and probably not even use my tag to locate me, as he most likely had my Jeep chipped long ago, so he knew where I was all the time. What do I do? How do I protect myself? *Oh my gosh! Am I chipped in some manner?* My brain was in hysterics, and I had to take in deep breaths and then release them slowly.

What could I do to stop Steve from tracking me? I'm running out of time. I couldn't go to the police as Steve was buddies with many of them, the same with the sheriff's office. *Calm down, Kim, and think! Calm down and rationalize this situation...*

Rob Caldwell – my high school classmate and personal lawyer, might be able to help. Rob, and his wife, Liza, never liked Steve, and Steve never liked Rob or Liza, so I was sure he would help me. Did I want to involve them in this craziness I was in or not?

Rob had sandy colored hair and blue eyes on his athletic frame of about six feet tall. His wife, Liza, is ultra skinny, athletic, at five feet, ten inches, with auburn hair and smoky violet eyes. *Yet did I want to involve them, and potentially get them killed??? What do I do?*

I drove to my art gallery, parked my *Jeep*, left my keys in the ignition, and my smart watch on the console. With both bags tossed over my shoulders, I ran all the way to Rob's office a few blocks away!

Trembling wildly, I made my way inside and found Rob preparing to leave for home, as it was lunchtime, and the office closed at noon on Fridays. One glance at me, and he was at my side. With one arm around my shoulders, he led me into his office.

I tried to speak, but no words came out of my open mouth, just like a fish out of water. Finally, I whispered to Rob, "lock the doors and turn off all of the office lights." Without question, he locked the office doors and turned the lights off.

The staff had already left for the day, so he was truly alone in the building. He helped me to a chair, and I collapsed in it as weariness consumed my entire being. With his arm around my shoulder and soothing words repeated, I managed to calm down enough to speak.

After I told Rob the true kind of work Steve did, and that I was set up to find my name at the top of his hit list this morning, his mouth opened in shock. As I continued telling Rob, with a tremble in my voice, what I had found, his look was grave.

By the time I told him of dinner last evening, the strange way that Steve and Gary had acted, and how Steve had been this morning, Rob believed me.

"We've got to keep you safe, Kim. What do you have with you and what have you done?" Rob asked in a gentle manner with concern written all over his face.

"I threw my cellphone down a ravine so Steve can't track me with it, and I ran into a store and bought three burner phones. My Jeep is at my art gallery with the keys in it, and I left my smart watch on the Jeep's console," as I took a deep breath to regain some composure and to think clearer.

"I also ran to the bank, withdrew $500,000 in cash, and I dropped my bank and credit cards in the bank's trash bin as I left the building," and a tear escaped my right eye and slid down to my chin. I was still trying to calm down and it was rough. "I kept only my driver's license and social security cards. Oh, Rob, this is truly real. How do I stop Steve from killing me?"

"That's a great start, Kim. So, what do you have with you now? Dump your bags on the carpet, empty them out, everything, and I will be right back. I must move my vehicle to an area where Steve can't see it. The door will stay locked, and I'll use the back entrance. You will be okay, take deep breaths in and out until I get back," Rob replied in a soothing tone of voice.

It felt like forever yet took only minutes before Rob stepped back inside his office. I was on the carpet with my bags dumped. A huge relief washed over and through me when I saw he was back safe.

We looked at what I had brought with me. Then Rob stated we needed more help, and he called his wife, Liza. Rob turned his mobile phone to speaker mode as he called his wife.

Liza answered, "Hi Hun! Are you leaving work now?"

"Hi Liza. No, not leaving just yet. I need you to follow some instructions to the absolute letter. Kim is in trouble, and I'll explain all when we see you. Do you understand so far?"

"Okay, Rob. Is Kim… okay?" Liza asked with concern in her voice.

"Liza dear, Kim is here, we don't have time for chatting, and I want to say the least bit on the phone. I need you to follow instructions to the letter after I hang up. Liza, I want you to get an Uber to take you to the store so you can purchase auburn hair dye and…"

"But…," Liza interrupted.

"Liza, please do what I ask and no further questions. First, you must leave your mobile at home – without question, leave it in the kitchen. Take an Uber to the store and have them wait for you while you're inside. Purchase the auburn hair dye and have the Uber driver bring you to the back entrance of my office. I will let you inside. All is dark inside the office, it will look closed, and my vehicle is parked else-where, but you will be fine. Do you understand?" Rob inquired with strained unease showing on his face.

"Yes, Rob. Calling Uber now and leaving my mobile in the kitchen. I love you!" Liza whispered in a nervous voice.

"I love you, too, Liza. See you soon, Babe."

What seemed like hours only took twenty minutes and Rob let Liza inside the back door. They walked into the office holding hands. Upon seeing Kim, Liza grabbed her in a hug and sat down beside her.

"Where is your mobile, Liza?" Rob asked outright.

"At home on the kitchen counter." Liza murmured as she looked Kim over for signs of injury.

"Great! Kim and I will tell you what the situation is at this time."

Throughout the storyline and events, Liza's face registered shock, anger, confusion, and disbelief. By the end, her expression was hard with anger, kept barely under control.

"Wow, Kim! I'm so sorry," as both women cried and hugged each other tightly. "I knew that Steve was bad, but I had no idea... I truly thought he was a private investigator. That Steve would put you on a hit list is so unbelievable, yet I've never noticed one single redeeming quality in him, not that we've met much. To me you two looked madly in love, and we were vermin to Steve..."

"Sorry to break this up, but first things first. What do you have with you, Liza? Rob questioned.

"I have my purse and a bottle of auburn hair dye," and she then handed both items to her husband.

Rob dumped her purse contents on the carpet, peered at the items closely, and found nothing traceable. "Here, Liza. There's nothing here that Steve can trace," Rob replied as she put her purse contents back in order.

"Okay, ladies, one step at a time so we don't mess things up, understood? Steve has no idea where the three of us are, as it looks like Liza is at home, in the kitchen making lunch, since her cellphone is on the counter, and it pings from there."

"Now, I must dump my cell phone in water so he can't trace it," and he promptly dropped his smart phone into a glass of water. "By the time thirty minutes go by, the phone will not be traceable or usable. Steve will question that, but we are still safe. Remember, we are safe, and I want to keep the three of us safe in the future."

The three of them looked at the contents of Kim's bag and purse. Rob studied both bags carefully and was satisfied that they were clean of any type of tracker.

"Hand both guns to me so I can look them both over," Rob requested. Finally, we slowly started going through the contents from each bag and my clothing was placed back in my backpack along with the water, and two of the burner phones alongside my pistol and ammo.

"I feel better now that you've looked at the items and checked both bags," Kim gave Rob a quick hug. "Thank you."

"Kim, your purse contents, I'm sorry but a great portion must be trashed. I can't see any trackers on your lipsticks but in the water, they must go just to be sure," and Rob helped Liza dump all of Kim's makeup, ink pens, all purse contents in the office sink, half filled with water.

"I want you to keep your cash, driver's license, and social security cards. Your nail file is fine, and of course the Ruger and ammo goes back into your purse." Rob explained.

Liza piped up, "Oh Kim, I have an idea. I want you to take my lipsticks, pens, and other purse essentials so you have what women carry. That way, you can bypass going into a store." Rob was impressed and told Liza she had a great idea!

"I will replace my mobile this afternoon, and I will keep my same number. That way Steve will think all is normal as far as Liza and I are concerned. The office is deserted, not unusual for a Friday afternoon, so if, and I do mean if, Steve drives past, the office will appear normal, even if Steve looks in the windows, he won't see anything unusual, and he can't see us at all." Rob resumed. Then he phoned Verizon to set him up with a replacement phone and he asked them to pre-activate it for him. They agreed.

"Now, Steve will receive pings from Kim's mobile and eventually locate it in the ravine, and then he will search for the Jeep and smart watch next. Liza, Kim parked her Jeep at the art gallery with the keys and smart watch in it, so that was a good way to leave it for Steve to find. He won't have any idea where Kim is," Rob continued, as he looked at both women.

"We've taken care of the phones and the vehicles for now, and I will drive my vehicle home later this afternoon. All will appear normal to Steve thus far," Rob murmured as he wracked his brain for the next step.

After a deep and slow breath, Rob added, "What we must do now, ladies, is to think like Steve. This won't be easy at all. Think about movies you watched and what the person did to thwart being found. This is all doable, not that thinking like a hit man is easy, but we can make this work!"

"The first steps are done, no one can trace Kim, and nothing looks out of the ordinary for either Liza or myself, except for my phone not pinging. We must take steps to keep up this charade of sorts," and both women nodded in the affirmative.

"Liza, take Kim into my private restroom, color her hair with the auburn hair dye, and make sure you do her eyebrows as well. Don't be afraid to turn on the lights, as there are no windows and nothing to be seen from the outside of my office building." Rob instructed both women.

With an afterthought he added, "Take your time and make sure all of Kim's hair is colored. Now would be a good time to add in some makeup changes to match the new hair color. We are safe here, don't worry."

Thirty minutes later, both Liza and Kim stepped back into the office and sat back down on the carpet. "How does Kim look to you, Rob," Liza queried anxiously.

"Kim's hair is the same shade as yours. Nice work. Do you think you could cut her hair, Liza? Give it a layered look or some such?" Rob handed scissors to his wife.

"Of course, I can! I was a stylist before we married, and I know how to make Kim's hair look completely different, similar to mine" and both ladies went back into the restroom.

Once again, both women came back into the office and Rob was impressed. The transformation of Kim was complete. Steve would never recognize her now. Of that, Rob was sure. As for the next steps to take, Rob was not so sure.

Chapter Three

"Where the hell is Kim? This game of cat and mouse was to be easy, not complicated. I know she overheard Gary Moore and me discussing our intel and plans to take out the President of the United States last night! It was rotten timing and I love Kim, but I'm a professional and so she must be taken out — fast! I must have given Kim too much of a head start. Kim is now a ticking time bomb that must be found and dealt with in short order before she leaks our plans!"

Steve decided to give Gary Moore a call to help find Kim ASAP! "Gary, glad to catch you. I need you. Come over so we can talk, okay?" Steve requested. "By the way, where is Nancy?"

"She went to the library to read up on babies and family planning all morning, Steve. Be right over."

Steve closed the door and both men went straight to Steve's office. "Kim knows, Gary. I must take her out, but she is hiding from me."

Gary's eyebrows raised. "Then she did overhear our conversation last evening. This must be tough on you, Steve, as Kim is your wife. That's unfortunate," Gary commiserated. "What have you done so far?"

"I traced her mobile phone to a ravine not far from here, and it appeared that she tossed it to throw me off track. Kim took both her 22-gauge automatic *Ruger* and her automatic 22-gauge revolver and extra ammo with her. Let's team up on this. Nip this as fast as we can."

"Okay, Steve. You do have a tracker on her Jeep, right?" Gary asked. "Where is her Jeep?"

"Coordinates show that the Jeep is at the art gallery and so is her smart watch. Jump in the *Land Rover* with me, okay? Grab your gear so we can fix this quickly, and be done with the whole sordid matter," replied Steve as he headed out the front door.

Once at the gallery, both men looked around and Kim's Jeep was there, with the keys in it and her smart watch lay on the console. After searching the gallery, both men knew Kim was elsewhere and time was running out.

"Who could possibly help Kim, to keep her safe?" Gary wondered aloud.

"Only two people, Gary. Rob Caldwell and his wife, Liza. I've tracked Rob's mobile to his law office and Liza is at home according to her mobile phone pings." Gary could read the tension in Steve's demeanor.

"Let's make sure Liza is actually home first as we need to know if she is aware of the situation." Gary knew that things had to be done in a systematic and orderly fashion, so all bases were covered. Time was of the essence.

After arriving at the Caldwell home, Steve knocked on the front door and no one answered. Both men decided to enter as they simply could not take any chances. Steve took the front entry and Gary took the back deck entrance.

A complete search told them that Liza was gone and that she knew! She'd left her mobile on the kitchen counter. "Liza is with Kim, I know it. That means Rob is involved as well. You drive, Gary, and I'll give you directions to his law office as we head that way." Steve's voice was calm and collected, a deadly voice, if one truly knew Steve. "First, I want to tap their home phone and I'll be quick about it."

Upon arrival, the law office was dark with no lights on. Rob's vehicle was nowhere to be found, and Gary suggested they back off, watch from a distance, and monitor both entrances. Using his special laptop, Steve noted Rob's phone no longer pinged at all! What did Rob do?

"Damn, Rob is smarter than I ever gave him credit for," Steve bellowed in anger. "My gut tells me the three of them are still inside his law office. It's only a matter of time now." Steve smirked.

Chapter Four

Kim, Liza, and Rob looked at his tablet and pondered the safest way to get Kim out of Boston. Rob reminded the women that all three were still safe in his office, and he went and grabbed cold bottles of water and protein bars from the breakroom.

Kim still had intense emotions but remained calm as she threw her wedding rings and jewelry in the trash can. Liza was rather fiery, her anger at Steve showing on her face. Rob presented a calm persona, even though he was anything but calm.

"I have a plan, but we must discuss it out and see if changes need to be made or additions to add in," responded Rob. All three studied the ways out of Boston on Rob's tablet.

The scenario started with Rob calling and making a reservation for Kim for that night, and for as long as she needed, at the Hartford Marriott in downtown Hartford, CT.

Kim had never been to Hartford, and she appreciated the effort Rob put forth to help her in this ghastly situation. Rob also paid for the hotel and told Kim she must check in under a code name, "Peaches" and only that name.

Rather than public transportation, all three decided Uber would be the safest. The Uber driver would pick up Kim from the back-office entrance.

"No, Rob, that won't work. I see Steve's Land Rover a block away and both entrances can be seen from where he is parked," Liza groaned as she sat back down on the carpet.

Rob took a quick peek and sat back down. "Time for a new plan, ladies. If Steve knows your phone is at home, Liza, but you aren't, he may think you're with me. Remember, we are safe here and no one knows for sure that we are here, or even if all three of us are here for that matter."

Aften mulling over ideas in his head, Rob announced a revision in the plan. "Kim, I need you to be strong. The same with you, Liza. All three of us must be stronger than we have ever been in our lives. We must remain strong and calm, act like usual, and this will work."

Both women sat next to each other as Rob continued, "In order to throw Steve off his 'game' we must play this cool, calm, and collected. First, I'm calling for a second Uber."

"I can tell that Rob has a great plan, Kim. This will work out; I know it will." Liza gave Kim a wobbly smile. After a few deep breaths, both watched Rob walk back to them.

Rob sat down with the women. "What we must do is befuddle Steve's mind and I have the exact trick to do it! Liza, I will walk you out to the first Uber, give you a hug and kiss, and the Uber driver will take you home. Do NOT look towards the Land Rover. I have security setting up at our home now, Liza, and you will be safe."

"But Rob…."

"No buts allowed. Hear me out, please, Kim? Liza will be safe, and I need you to be brave and strong so we can pull this off. After a few minutes, I will leave through the back door and you will stay in my office, nice and safe. I promise that you will be safe. Do you trust me?" Rob questioned Kim.

Liza and Kim looked at each other and nodded in the affirmative.

"I will walk across the street to Verizon and pick up my pre-activated replacement mobile with my same number. All the while, I'll be monitoring the back door, and I will ignore Steve's vehicle. Once my phone is in my hand, I will make it look like I've called someone, and it should be pinging on Steve's laptop. That way, he will think my phone messed up earlier and with the replacement, he will think I know nothing! This is crucial for the plan to work." Rob stated and looked both women in the eye.

"Steve will think I simply replaced my phone. I will act like I'm talking on the phone as I walk to the corner store and go inside. Steve will think the law office is a dead end, as he would never, ever, suspect that I would leave Kim inside, alone, in my office – not with both of us gone in a normal manner. Are you both with me still?"

Both women said yes, with determined, yet fearful expressions on their faces.

"I will be near the front of the store perusing a display of winter gloves as it is November and cold this far north, and that will give Steve pause to wonder where you are. Now, I won't be on my phone, but I can still see the Land Rover from the corner of my eye. When the coast is clear and Steve is no longer watching the office, I will call you on your first burner phone, Kim."

"Okay, Rob. How do I leave the office in a safe way?" Kim asked with a nervous and trembly tone in her voice.

"The second Uber will pull up at the back entrance, and I will also be back with you in the office by then. The Uber driver will help you inside and he will then head for Hartford, CT via I-90 and then I-84 until he gets you to the hotel. Understood?"

Kim nodded yes.

"Great! The Uber driver has been forewarned, and paid handsomely, to take you out of Boston using my instructions. He also has my mobile number," Rob sighed. "This is doable and safe, please trust me." Kim was shivering in fright and Liza wrapped her arms around her in comfort, and spoke in a soft, soothing tone in her ear.

"Kim, you must trust me on this please. We don't want to lose you, and if Steve suspects that either Liza or I are involved, he will take us ALL out. We know that will happen. The goal is to keep all three of us alive and safe. Okay? Are you both still with me?" Rob implored, and both women nodded yes.

"The Uber driver has been instructed to take you straight to the Hartford Marriott downtown. Once there, the driver will accompany you to the check-in desk. Using the alias of "Peaches", Kim will check in and be taken to her room accompanied by security. I've paid extra for security to monitor the hall where your suite is located. This is doable and Steve simply won't know where you are! I'm positive he won't know."

Once behind her locked door, Kim was to use her burner phone number one and call Rob and Liza at home, on their home phone, and not their mobiles. Liza had come up with the idea of using the home phone rather than mobiles as it would be safer, and not trackable, no pings to track. By then, Rob would have the rest of the plan figured out.

Chapter Five

"*D*amn!" yelled Steve as he watched Liza leave in an Uber, and Rob crossed the street, before going inside the Verizon store.

"Evidently, Rob picked up a replacement phone from Verizon as his new mobile now pings, and neither Liza nor Rob looked in our direction. We must do something different! Kim's not here! Oh no! Kim won't get away! Not now, not ever!" Steve snarled out ferociously.

Steve took over driving, and he drove lightning fast to get home and strategize with Gary on the next steps. Time was not on their side. Now this simple mission took on an urgency he'd not anticipated, at all.

Once home, they set up the equipment to monitor both Rob and Liza's mobiles and their home phone was already tapped. No chatter, nothing except for Rob's phone pinging as he drove home, and of course Liza's phone still pinging from home.

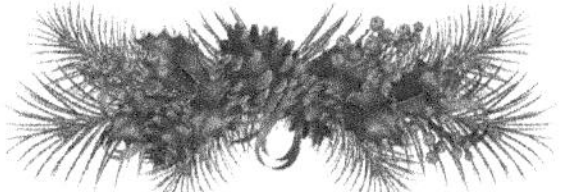

"We will next speak after you're settled at the hotel in Hartford, CT, and by then I will have the rest of the plans laid out. Since it's the middle of the afternoon, and before rush hour you should be at the hotel in less than 2 1/2 hours, so that's not a bad drive and the Uber driver knows that this is extremely important and dangerous. He will keep you safe as I paid extra for this service." Rob continued.

"When you call, Kim, we'll discuss what type of vehicle you want me to line up for you and the rest of the details. Breakfast will be delivered to your room via security. Order whatever you feel up to eating and make sure you eat plenty of protein. That goes double for dinner this evening."

"We've got her, Gary!" Steve slammed his headphones on his desk. "The tap on Rob's home phone worked like a charm. Before we do anything about Rob and Liza, we must get to Kim first. She's at the Hartford Marriott downtown in Hartford, CT. Let's go now! Kim has no idea that we know where she is, and that will work out perfect in our favor," Steve sneered. *Little did Steve know that his own home phone had been tapped and the entire conversation was heard by none other than the CIA!*

En route and just as Steve drove over I-395, the *Land Rover* hit black ice and lost traction. The vehicle went into a skid on the slick pavement, flipped over the railing and ended wheels up on I-385. Steve and Gary both died on impact.

Steve had not realized that he had been followed the entire time he was driving toward Hartford. Two men from the CIA (Central Intelligence Agency) had been tailing him. The CIA was first on the scene of the wreck. After making sure the men were dead, they quickly and efficiently took fingerprints from both men for analysis.

The CIA had to know if they, indeed, had the right men for this Top-Secret assignment. The electronic results came back and BAM! The two most wanted people on the CIA's list came back positive! The prints had been run through INTERPOL and the international fingerprint database known as AFIS (Automated Fingerprint Identification System).

Ambulances and patrol men arrived, but the CIA took full control of the scene. The President was safe! His would-be assassins were dead! The bodies of both men were taken, under guard, to a morgue run by the OCME (Office of Chief Medical Examiner) in Washington, DC, for forensics.

The director of the CIA, Richard Cook, took over the Top-Secret assignment after being briefed by the agents who had trailed Steve and Gary. Richard Cook answered directly to the Director of National Intelligence, although he did brief the President on occasion.

The NSA is led by the Director of the National Security Agency (DIRNSA), who also serves as Chief of the Central Security Service (CHCSS) and Commander of the United States Cyber Command (USCYBERCOM) and is the highest-ranking military official of these organizations. The DOD (U.S. Department of Defense) housed the CIA and the National Guard.

Capturing both Steve and Gary was a huge feather in their cap. Yet more work had to be done. They needed all the intel Gary and Steve had in their respective homes. They needed to know who the handler was for both men. That handler could still get the President killed!

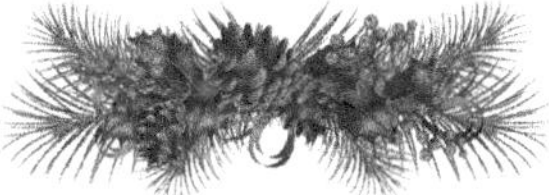

Nancy had been worried for hours. Gary wasn't picking up her calls to him, and before she knew it, her front doorbell rang. She answered right away only to find two men wearing CIA jackets standing outside.

"How bad?" Nancy breathed out the words as she knew Gary must have been in an accident of some type. The CIA agents took Nancy inside and Special Agent Thompson informed her that Gary had been killed in an accident along with Steve. The vehicle had hit black ice and flipped over. "Why? Why Gary? We were going to start a family," Nancy shouted as she cried out. "Does Kim know about Steve?"

"Agents are headed toward Kim as we speak." Agent Thompson replied. Nancy peered out the window at Steve and Kim's dark house.

"Please get your coat and purse, Mrs. Moore. You must come with us now." Nancy complied as despair and fear registered on her face. She didn't want to be alone.

"Liza! Come quick, there's been an accident and it's on the news. The CIA is at the scene!" Rob called out to his wife in the kitchen, and she ran and sat down beside him. The scene of the accident was unreal. Both Steve and Gary dead. Killed instantly when the vehicle hit the freeway below.

"Oh, Rob, why did it happen this way? Kim must be told. I'll give her a call now."

"Kim? It's Liza. Have you seen the early evening news?"

"No. What happened?" Kim asked, as she sat down on the sofa in her room. As gently as she could, Liza told Kim that Steve and Gary were both killed in an accident earlier after hitting black ice and flipping over. Shock slammed Kim in the gut, and she dropped the phone.

Rob and Liza decided that it would be best that Kim not be left alone, and Liza told Kim they were leaving for Hartford shortly and would meet her at the hotel, but Kim had dropped the phone and didn't hear this part.

When Kim answered the door to her room, she was shocked to see Rob and Liza. All three hugged each other, with tears for what could have been, and relief for what God had prevented. Two CIA agents interrupted them and introduced themselves as Senior Agent Hughes and Agent Thomas.

Rob ushered the agents into the room, and they all sat down around the hotel suite's sitting area.

Senior Agent Hughes delivered the uncomfortable and shocking news. "Kim, your husband was number one on the CIA's most wanted list and Gary was number two," as Kim broke into fresh tears. So much had happened in the span of a few hours.

Agent Hughes continued, "I know this must be difficult to hear, but this is mandatory, so you are aware of what the CIA is doing right now," as he passed a tissue box to Kim and Liza.

"Currently, the CIA has a search warrant for your and Gary's homes, in Beacon Hill, and they are there now doing a complete raid, taking every scrap of evidence and electronic equipment they can find. The warrant justified the CIA to seize all evidence." Agent Hughes looked at the three of them, Kim, Rob, and Liza, before continuing.

Kim was shell shocked, and Rob was angry that Steve had been such a vile man. Liza had no words, she simply sat back and listened with disbelief on her face.

"I need you to pack your bags now, as all three of you will be taken to Washington, DC. None of you are in trouble. We know from our intel that Steve and Gary are the only ones responsible, and the plan had been to assassinate the President. What we don't know is the name and location of the agent handler extraordinaire, who put out this hit job on the President nor the reason behind it."

Liza helped Kim pack up, and the CIA assisted in taking all luggage down to their waiting, dark tinted windowed SUV.

Chapter Six

It was a solemn morning the next day, as Kim, Liza, Rob, and Nancy Moore, who was already present in the room, finished with the CIA's and Homeland Security's interviews.

Following the interviews, all four were flown back to Boston on a military plane and taken to their respective homes.

Neither Kim nor Nancy wanted to be alone, so Rob went in with Kim and Liza went into Nancy's home with her. Kim and Nancy were shocked at the scenes before them in their respective homes.

Tom, Kim's landscaper/caretaker was already inside her home with Susan, her housekeeper, as they had seen the tragic news the evening before, and the CIA had searched Tom's home during the raid, since it was part of the property belonging to the estate that Steve and Kim owned.

At the Moore home, Nancy fell to her knees and sobbed. Liza helped her up and they walked next door to Kim's house.

"I can't stay here, I just can't," Kim screamed, and Nancy agreed. She simply couldn't stay in the home that she and Gary had created, and Kim was beyond devastated with all that happened in one single day, not to mention the state of her house.

Susan tried to comfort both women, and Kim stated in a matter-of-fact tone, "I will not stay in this house again. Never." It was decided that everyone would go to Rob and Liza's home and discuss things out as to what the women wanted to do.

At Rob's house, Kim insisted, "I will NOT have anything to do with Steve's burial, and I refuse to attend the service. I won't plan it and Steve was a stranger to me. I never knew the real man, only a façade! Let the CIA deal with Steve's body!" Nancy agreed and said she felt the same way about Gary, and she planned to get the heck out of Dodge once she knew where she was going! She never wanted to live in her home again. Rob cautioned both women not to make hasty decisions and to give a lot of thought in the direction they wanted their lives to move forward.

Life has a way of working itself out. Kim replaced her original phone and number, her hair was turned back into her curly blonde color, and, in the end, both women sold their homes to Tom and Susan, who were married three weeks later. The couple planned to remodel and open both homes, and the cottage bungalow behind Kim's old home, as high-end Airbnb's.

PART II

Chapter Seven

$\mathcal{B}$oth Kim and Nancy decided to pack up and move, together. The movers had packed up the items Nancy wanted to keep, and the rest was left with the sale of her house.

Kim had her home art studio, her art, and sculptures, as well as her art gallery packed up by professional movers. Most furniture was left in her old Beacon Hill house as Kim had zero desire for memories purely based on a lie. She sold every piece of jewelry that Steve had given her – at low prices, and only kept pieces she had bought for herself.

Was life easy? No. But they moved onward, in a new and different direction, far from what they left behind, and the relationships that were as fake as... money, trust, banking, they reflected throughout the drive, and noted a tiny bit of healing was happening the further away from Boston they drove.

Both received life insurance benefits, in generous amounts (the men died in a vehicular accident, after all), and both decided to start new lives in Colorado.

The women planned to eventually settle in Evergreen, CO. Specifically, the Heart of Evergreen which has a lake, eclectic shops and dining, lovely homes in well-established forests, and elk that lived there year-round. The process would not go terribly fast since they had yet to view any rentals or homes for sale on the market. That would come with time.

En route to Colorado, and taking turns driving, the 30-hour drive took them four days to make. Although it snowed off and on throughout the drive, the Jeep handled the weather with finesse.

The women reminisced about what had happened, and they cried at times. It was only natural to do so. By the time they hit the Colorado state line, talk was of Colorado, and not of their old lives.

"We should arrive around 2pm at my dear high school friend, Sarah Leawood's, Lakewood, CO, home. It was kind and generous of Sarah to give us a place to stay during our search for new homes," as Kim described the family of their hostess to Nancy, who sat up front and next to her in the Jeep that she loved. Nancy had planned to purchase a new vehicle in Colorado.

"Now, Sarah, had a rough first marriage and her ex was extremely brutal to her in every way possible. She has a son, Danny, a Boy Scout, and she's a wonderful ER trauma nurse, truly a special nurse, and had been inducted into STTI (Sigma Theta Tau International), the largest international nursing honor society in the world, when she was close to graduation."

"Sarah sounds like the kind of nurse I'd want to have helping me in the hospital," Nancy commented. "I know we'll be friends in no time. You grimaced. Does your back hurt, Kim?"

"Not too bad, just rearranging my lumbar support. Sarah is 30, and I must tell you about the horrific loss of Sarah's younger son, Simon, from the effects of treating aggressive cancer. Sarah and Danny talk about Simon as they want to keep him remembered and never to become forgotten," Kim added.

"Oh, my goodness," Nancy replied as she grabbed more tissues for her fresh tears. Nancy was sad to learn about this, yet she thought she might be able to help Sarah and Danny deal with their loss, since she had taken college classes on bereavement, in her prior life, and was certified.

Kim continued, "Danny is 12 now, and has ADHD - attention deficit hyperactivity disorder, but he's as smart as a whip in most areas.

Danny has short, darker hair, and cobalt blue eyes like his mom. You will love them, Nancy," as Kim filled her in with background information to help her feel like she knew their hosts and would be more comfortable.

"Furthermore, Sarah works as a trauma nurse in the ER, and she places PICC lines (peripherally inserted central catheters – the tip is usually left two or three centimeters away from the right side of the heart, in a large vein just above the heart), when needed," Kim added. "Why I remember this PICC line information is beyond me," she wondered aloud.

"Sarah is married to a trauma doctor, Dr. Aaron Leawood, 33, and a friend since her high school days. Sarah has wavy blond hair with cobalt blue eyes, and a trim figure. Dr. Leawood is tall, around six feet, four inches with dark hair and eyes to match, and rather athletic. Lisa is eight, I think, with curly blonde hair and blue eyes."

"Dr. Leawood's first wife left him while he was in medical school. Then his girlfriend got pregnant, so he married her for the baby's sake. That marriage was doomed from the start, and as soon as she gave birth, she left and filed for divorce. Their daughter, Lisa, stayed with Aaron as his ex-wife wanted nothing to do with her own child."

"How could she…" Nancy was stupefied and shook her head back and forth in a no gesture. How a mother could give up her baby as soon as it was born stymied Nancy, who had yearned to start a family in her prior life. Truly, this world was made up of so many types of people, and more than one thinks and focuses on themselves only, or they have abortions so they can further their careers. Some Hollywood types and such a shame. They could afford birth control! Other people love and help all. Nancy was determined to have a family someday.

"They do have a housekeeper, Sadie Edwards is her name, and she lives in a cottage behind their home. His mom, Alice, has her own small home behind the main house as well, especially built for her as Aaron's sister, Cindy, down in Colorado Springs, became toxic to all of them, and he wanted his mother close by him. Honestly, Alice loves being there and seeing both grandchildren as much as she likes. Oh, and she is big on reading books! I almost forgot that. I think she has a book club." As Kim remembered, a smile lit up her face, Nancy saw the look and knew they were going down the right path.

"I know you will love Sarah and her family. Now, what else can I tell you, so you don't feel like they are strangers?" Kim queried as she drove south down I-25.

"I don't know, but this is surely a crash course on learning so much about our hosts. I feel more comfortable now, staying with them. Thank you, Kim." Both women smiled at each other, content in the direction their lives were headed.

Chapter Eight

It was close to 3pm when they arrived at Sarah and Aaron's Lakewood home. Large feathery flakes of snow had been softly falling for the last half hour.

Danny and Lisa bounded out of the house with their parents following. Sarah gave a squeal as she hugged Kim tightly, followed by Aaron. Kim introduced Nancy, and she received warm hugs, and both were welcomed into their home. The luggage was brought in by Aaron.

After settling inside the spacious living room of the beautiful timbered and river rock home of their hosts, everyone found a place to sit not far from the roaring fire.

Sadie brought in hot cocoa and cookies as refreshments and the children sat near the fire smiling and happy; they were excited to have new company staying with them in the house, and the cocoa and cookies.

"Oh! I'd forgotten how gorgeous your home is! From the front it's postcard perfect with the timbers, river rock, small lake, and stream, both cottages, outbuildings, and white mini lights aglow in the softly falling snow." Kim spoke first, a look of amazement upon her face.

"I second what Kim said even though I'm seeing it for the first time." Nancy smiled at their hosts.

Sarah smiled at both women, whom she considered her friends already, as she knew Kim, and was given background information on Nancy before they'd left Boston.

Aaron was ahead of the game. "You each have your own bedroom with a bathroom across the hall. When you are ready, Sarah and I will show you around."

After clearing out the mugs and empty plates that had held peanut butter cookies, and rinsing them in the kitchen sink, the tour began as Sadie loaded the dishwasher, and went back to checking on the roast beef dinner that was baking.

The kitchen was cheery and evoked a sense of home, a sense of arriving, a sense of safety, and a feeling of finding home at last. Oak cabinets and granite counter tops matched the island in the middle. Black and chrome appliances fit in perfectly.

Through the floor to ceiling picture windows, two small cottages, some outbuildings, and a small, but entirely lovely, lake fed by a small stream, gave Kim and Nancy an 'aha' moment through the gently falling snow scene. Thanksgiving was only a week away and they had much to be thankful for, safety, a roof over their heads, keeping their heads in their prior lives, family, friends, and new friends.

At that moment, Dr. Leawood was paged to do a consultation for Dr. Paul Smith, a neurosurgeon, at the hospital he worked at in Lakewood. Even though Dr. Leawood was primarily an ER doctor, he did work with neurosurgery prior to the ER, and he was best friends with Dr. Smith. He knew if Dr. Smith paged him, it was important, indeed.

"Okay, Sarah, ladies, sorry, but I must go and see what Dr. Smith needs. I'll be back home before dinner." After bundling up in a parka and snow gear, and giving Sarah a quick kiss, Aaron left for the hospital.

"Let's begin the tour! This is where all things winter goes," Sarah smiled as they walked into the mud room. "In here is where all our outdoor gear such as snowshoes, ski equipment, ice skates, and heavy outerwear are kept. We have a lot of equipment for winter sports, which means we probably have pieces that fit both of you. Do either of you ski?"

"I do," Kim smiled as she looked over the well-maintained gear. "So does Nancy, we both love to ski. The slopes were close to us in Boston…Oh Nancy, I'm so sorry."

"Don't worry, Kim, we are bound to mention parts of our old lives from time to time," and, as a tear ran down her cheek slowly, Nancy regained composure.

"Okay, time for a group hug," and Sarah opened her arms wide. The three women hugged each other, knowing that each of them had overcome struggles of one sort or another and that they would all be fine; He knew the path forward and all three silently prayed.

"Shall we continue?" Sarah led the women to the laundry room as she explained that all summer sports gear had their own shed behind the main house.

"This is our laundry room, and you are free to use it as you wish." Sarah smiled and led the women toward the door leading to a deck outside. "This part of our deck receives extra muddy and grimy gear, before stepping inside the mud room."

From there, Sarah led the women back up the hall and through the open kitchen to the dining room. Exposed beams in the vaulted ceiling gave warmth to the room, which was dominated by a large gleaming rectangular pecan dining table that sat 12 people with ease. Matching chairs surrounded the table that was decorated with candles and autumn decorations, gourds, small pumpkins, and fake pine branches.

The soft lighting above the table leant an air of coziness to the overall room. Family pictures graced the walls, and a set of bay windows surrounded a breakfast/reading nook, which easily seated five or six people. Soft rose-colored cushions created a perfect place to read, snack, drink coffee, or daydream. Oak herringbone wood flooring completed the spacious room.

Sarah led the women through a curved arch and into the main living room they had been in earlier when they arrived. "I will show you our master bedroom suite next," and she led the women through another arched doorway and down a hall.

The first door on the right was the master bedroom with an ensuite and a lovely fireplace. A king sized, carved, dark mahogany, four poster bed dominated the room, with matching carved tables on either side of the bed that was covered in a plush autumn duvet, and decorative pillows. Two walk-in closets completed the master suite and the oak walls held photos of happy family times.

"Further down the hall and on the right is Aaron's den," Sarah pointed out. "Please don't use his room as Aaron makes notes regarding patients now and then, and patient privacy is highly important."

Across the hall was a full bath decorated in autumn colors for the season. "And now we come to the playroom," Sarah smiled as she showed the way to the open room filled with books and toys for Danny and Lisa; both children playing a board game and laughing.

"Aaron and I like having the children near us when they are playing. We can hear them laugh and giggle, yet still watch a movie or listen to music as we discuss our day at work or events around the world. This room is called *Danny and Lisa*, and the kids love having the room named after them." Sarah smiled down at the children, her heart full of love.

"I caught that yawn, Nancy. Why don't I show you to your rooms so you can rest up and the rest of the tour will continue later, okay?" Sarah asked. "Follow me, please."

Back in the entryway, Sarah led the women up a large, carved, and curved, mahogany staircase with the balustrade decorated in fake pine boughs and autumn décor. The stairway was covered in light brown carpeting.

"The first door on the right is your room, Kim, and the second door on the right is yours, Nancy. Both rooms have full beds and are furnished like each other with pecan beds and dressers, tables, light carpeting, and writing desks. The closets are over to the side, and we truly want you to feel like this is your home, because it is, and for as long as you need it."

"Thank you," Kim and Nancy replied in unison as each went into their rooms and closed the doors.

Chapter Nine

Kim sank down upon the cozy duvet on her bed. The muted rose tones gave a feminine air to the room's ambiance. Seeing her luggage, she stood back up and unpacked. Once done she lay down on her bed and dozed off, trying to rest her low back pain that nothing yet had been able to help.

Nancy loved the shades of soft blue her room was decorated in, and she went to work on her luggage right away. Once done, she sat down in a rocking chair, and contemplated her future and that of Kim.

Kim awoke when she heard squeals coming from the children in the hallway. Stepping out of her room, she saw Nancy with Danny and Lisa, and Sarah was close behind them.

"I'm sorry if the children woke you, they are rather excited and want you to see their rooms. On the left is Danny's room and his is just the way a boy of his age wants to have it. He has a full-size bed, and he loves all things racing, and race cars and so his room is decorated half with racing décor and the rest is full of Boy Scout memorabilia, trophies, badges, pinewood derby cars, and collections from scouting events."

"See my desk, Kim? Isn't it cool! I have a racecar clock and check out my posters!" Danny grinned and Kim smiled down at him.

"The children share a bathroom between their rooms." Sarah continued. "It's a full bath and both doors stay open unless one is in the bathroom. So, they have privacy and personal space, and through that door is Lisa's room."

"Look at my bed, Nancy! Do you like unicorns? I love them," Lisa beamed. Evidently, both kids had taken to Nancy right away.

"Unicorns are fantastic," she replied with a smile on her face.

"Lisa and unicorns go hand in hand. She loves her unicorn sleigh bed and décor. As you can see, she has her own desk for schoolwork and drawing." Sarah smiled down at Lisa.

A children's book, *Unicorn Dreams by Mary L. Schmidt,* lay on the desk. Scattered around the room and on the walls, different unicorns in various colors commanded attention due to the vibrancy. A perfect room for a little girl.

"Further down the hall we have two more guest bedrooms, and they are occupied by Sadie and Alice when the weather is bad. That way they stay safe in our home and do not walk on slick ice or in deep snow to their cottages. At the end of the hall is another full bath and a door leading up to the attic. We won't go up there now, but we have left the attic fully open, and two walls have two dormer windows each on opposite sides. The storage up there was needed like most attics are." Sarah pointed down the hall.

"That's the tour ladies. We do have a basement and we store seasonal items and mementos down there. Access is a door near the pantry, in the kitchen. Special mementos and such are stored down there, and we have a second laundry room as well."

"Daddy's home," squealed Lisa as the front door opened and Aaron walked inside.

"Dad!" Danny called out as he ran down the stairs followed by the women. This was the first time Danny had called Aaron, 'DAD'. No one made a big deal over it, but hearts swelled with love all around.

"Hi, Sweetheart," Aaron gave his daughter a huge hug, followed by Danny, who, at his age, still liked to have hugs now and then, when he was excited, and Sarah with a brief kiss. "Something cooking smells good."

Danny was a little insecure, still. He desperately wanted Aaron to know that he loved him, and he felt like Aaron was his real dad.

Aaron understood Danny's feelings with his history, and loved Danny like his own son. Finally calling him "Dad" after two years melted Aaron's heart.

"Right on time, you are, for dinner." Sadie replied as she headed back into the kitchen to finish meal prep.

"Wash up, kids," Sarah shooed Danny and Lisa into the bathroom before going to lay out dinnerware and utensils on the table. This time the table was set for eight, which included Sadie and Alice, who'd just come in the back door.

Aaron brought the large beef roast to the table and Sarah and Sadie placed potatoes and cooked carrots on the table. Rolls and butter sat waiting as Sadie brought in the final dish, a large apple streusel pie. Aaron and Sarah served the children and they all dug in to eat.

After dinner, the kids took their baths and put on pajamas before coming back into the living room. It was dark out, especially with the home located on the front range of the Rocky Mountains.

Back in the living room, everyone sat down near the fireplace, but Danny, ever inquisitive, peeked out the bay windows in the dining nook area, then called out. "The snow has stopped and come see the deer!"

In the moonlight, a female doe and two fawns stood in the snow, rummaging around for food beneath the snow. The family quietly watched the deer when a hare ran into view. The hare was off in the pines before they knew it. A perfect ending to the nice day.

Chapter Ten

*A*aron left for work early the next day, and Sarah had taken a personal day off so she could drive Kim and Nancy around the area and up into Evergreen.

Sarah drove a white Cadillac Escalade, and the children, Kim, and Nancy climbed into the vehicle. Grandma Alice would be picking the kids up from school today while the women were in Evergreen.

"Since we had the fresh snow yesterday, and the sky is clear today, I thought to take you up Lookout Mountain so you can see the continental divide." Sarah knew the view would be fantastic as her family had been up there more times than she could count.

Near the top, Kim and Nancy looked through the snowy pines and saw the divide in all its majesty. Many "oohs" and "aahs" were heard as all three of them pointed out different parts of the divide and some deer ran past them into the brush. Snapping cell phone pictures right and left, they all took time to enjoy the serenity of the moment.

Lookout Mountain is a great spot for nature and outdoor lovers. One can hike a 4.4-mile trail or drive to the top as the road is open year-round, since private homes were located on either side of the drive up from Golden, CO, and the Drive down to I-70.

Lookout Mountain sits at over 7,300 feet above Golden." Sarah commented, "but get this! If you look, you can see four different states including Utah, New Mexico, Arizona, and Colorado."

"What a view! Kim exclaimed, with Nancy following suit.

"We've missed out on a lot of gorgeous views in different states when we lived in Boston. But now things are the opposite!" Nancy burst out with a huge grin on her face. "Hello Colorado! We've arrived!" The women laughed.

Hopping back inside the Escalade, Kim explained that the Buffalo Bill Museum and Grave, at the top, required an admission fee, but admission to the park is free. William F. "Buffalo Bill" Cody died in 1917 and was buried in Lookout Mountain Park. Apparently, Cody made sure his wife and friends knew where he wanted his grave to be, and he wanted to overlook the Great Plains where he had spent much of his life.

Once they reached I-70, Sarah drove in a westward direction, until she took a left onto 74, and the outstanding views of the newer areas of Evergreen came into view. Sarah continued south on Evergreen Parkway until they arrived in the Heart of Evergreen, the original town, and a frozen over lake was in front of them.

Sarah swung a right on Upper Bear Creek Road, and they slowly drove past a herd of elk grazing near the road as Kim and Nancy took pictures on their cell phones.

"They are huge! Look at those antlers! And they don't run away from us!" Kim noticed and turned to their hostess.

"The elk don't mind photos taken, they are used to that, but don't for a minute think you are safe outside and near them. They are wild, and unpredictable animals, especially during mating season and when they have new babies out." Sarah cautioned the ladies.

"Those who live here walk around the lake often, and they walk near elk at times, but never during the rut or when babies are with their mothers. The elevation of Evergreen is 7,220 feet," Sarah smiled. "Not only do the elk live here year-round, so do osprey, bald eagles, great blue herons, and other species. The lake is full of trout and many fish for trout all year long."

"The lake itself is 55 acres, and as for water sports, this lake allows for year-round fishing, boating, and sailing in the summer, and ice skating and hockey in the winter months." Sarah explained. "Absolutely no swimming allowed for man or beast, meaning dogs. The Colorado health department issued a guidance that discouraged body contact in water supply reservoirs because of water quality concerns. This lake is a reservoir started and owned by the City of Denver."

Finally, they reached the Evergreen Lakehouse and parked in the parking lot. Sarah explained that the Evergreen Lakehouse was a perfect venue for all things weddings, parties, and events of most any type, and any time of the year. The rustic mountain lake house has 5,000 feet of entertaining space and the house itself was built with Montana lodgepole logs. Lots of space for indoor and outdoor events and the deck offers more venue area and gorgeous views of the lake and surroundings.

"Furthermore, I must show you the truly quaint shops, art galleries, eateries, and the scenery that make up the Heart of Evergreen," Sarah continued.

"Art galleries you say?" Queried Kim. "I'm looking to set up a new art gallery here. A realtor is on my to do list for a gallery spot and a new-to-me home, and Nancy wants a home here, too. She even promised to work in my gallery, I mean, we have money from life insurance, selling our homes in Boston, and all of that, but Nancy wanted something to do so she said yes!!! My best friend from Boston said yes to work in my gallery."

"Why don't we go stop in at the Bear Creek Café? They are open for breakfast, brunch, lunch, and they have a coffee shop? It's right over there on the north side of the lake." Sarah inquired and pointed at the café.

"Oh yes, I'm famished. What a great idea, Sarah. While we are at it, we can get a better feel of Evergreen." Nancy commented.

The women were seated at a booth looking out at the snow and ice-covered lake with a few people skating on the ice area, cleared of snow, near the Lakehouse. After perusing the menu, all three decided to have the Smoked Salmon Tartine with Lemon Dill Cream Cheese, and the traditional accompaniments, with a basic side salad. Sarah chose an Americano as she loved espresso, Kim chose a Pumpkin Spice Latte, and Nancy finally decided on a Caramel Macchiato.

It was getting a bit late in the day when they headed back home loaded with flyers and realtors' business cards. Kim's lower back was hurting, and Nancy placed an icy hot patch over the spot before they left.

Chapter Eleven

*A*aron and Sarah had left earlier for work and Sarah dropped the children off at school on her way in. Her new hours made that possible and she was grateful. Alice was set to pick them up after school was over. Both children would be on a school holiday until the Monday after Thanksgiving. Thanksgiving was this coming Thursday!

Sadie and Alice were in the breakfast/reading nook having coffee. Upon seeing Kim and Nancy, Sadie mentioned that a new pot of coffee demanded their attention and must be drunk, as she whipped up two ham and cheese omelets for their guests.

Seated at the table, conversation flowed freely and easily as they ate. After clearing away the dishes, the brochures and realtor cards came out. Kim reached for a shiny circular and, "Ouch!" She'd stretched too far and now her lumbar spine was hurting with greater intensity.

"I'll grab you an icy hot patch. Be right back," Nancy called out on her way to get a patch.

"What is up with your back, Kim? I can tell you have scoliosis, but did you hurt your back in some way?" Alice wanted to help, if she could, and if she couldn't, she knew one way to get Kim help. And that would be through her son, Aaron, referring Kim to see Dr. Paul Smith, a neurosurgeon, on staff at the hospital.

"My back has been bothering me for several years now, and it's getting worse. I've tried various methods to help my situation, but they have been dismal failures. Thanks for that patch, Nancy". Kim smiled in her response.

"No problem at all my friend. Feel like looking at brochures" Nancy asked as she looked at Kim carefully for signs of pain.

"Oh, yes, much better. Thanks. Have espresso, will peruse! That will be my motto for today."

Perusing the homes for sale and apartments to rent, one caught her eye right away. "I don't believe what I'm reading. Maybe Jesus meant for me to see this offer," Kim exclaimed as she opened her laptop to get a better view of the home in Evergreen surrounded by pines.

"Believe it or not, the word elevator caught my attention first," as she logged in to the realtor's website.

"Listen to this, heck, come look at the slides of the home with me."

Gathered in the reading nook they started to read the description and looked at the slide show presented to them. The home was named "Pine Lodge", and it was built in 2020. A beautiful log and river rock home with a fire-resistant faux shake shingle roof, featuring three beds and four baths, with each bedroom complete with its own private bathroom.

The main floor had floor to ceiling windows in the great room, and paired with its open concept, created a comfortable, connected, and luxurious feel. "Oh! It comes with custom log furniture!" Kim said with excitement, "Look at this. I know exactly where to put my large screen television!"

"We are, Kim, we are," Nancy laughed while Sadie decided to make a new pot of coffee, and Alice grabbed four butter croissants with napkins.

The hardwood floors shone, and the ceilings were vaulted. The fireplace had stone surrounds, and the window treatments complemented the look. The kitchen featured slab granite counters with a slab granite kitchen island. A large walk-in pantry was next to a personal elevator that covered all three floors.

"My back would love that elevator," remarked Kim and they all laughed knowing that it truly would. The kitchen came with a stainless-steel self-cleaning oven, dishwasher, refrigerator, and a built-in microwave. The dark wood cabinetry throughout the kitchen, and into the dining room completed the look of wood, pines, and luxurious mountain living.

Off the main living room, sliding glass doors led out to a red wood deck equipped with a picnic table, benches, six Adirondack chairs and two kid size Adirondacks, along with an outdoor grill area. The deck was basically ground level with outstanding views of the forest and mountain tops.

Since the home was built into the side of a mountain, one could enter via the two-car garage that opened into the bottom floor that contained a washer, dryer, and mud room. From there the choice of using a stairway or the elevator led up to the main and upper floors.

The next slide showed a large, yet cozy, office/den with a fireplace as well, this one a gas fireplace. Back down the hall was a guest bathroom with granite counters, a porcelain sink, and a shower/tub combo.

The master bedroom was on the main floor as well and it looked sinfully delicious, including both his and her closets, and a full bath with jacuzzi. Knobby pine furniture and a king size bed with plush, muted shades of rose and light blue made for a cozy feel. Above the bed was a five-blade ceiling fan. The deck was also accessible from the master bedroom, and the home had a smart lock system for contactless entry and exit.

The upper floor contained two bedrooms with private baths, two skylights that let in sunshine and a library/playroom combo. The knobby pine shelves on two walls complemented the sitting area. The HOA (Homeowner's Association) included trash, snow removal, and mowing.

"I'm calling the realtor now to see if it's still available, and, if so, schedule a viewing." Kim dialed the number listed and Pam Wilkins answered on the third ring. An appointment to view the home was made for tomorrow, Saturday afternoon at 2pm.

Alice left to pick up the children from school. Both children were excited to be on Thanksgiving break for the next nine days.

After viewing the home in Evergreen, Kim decided to buy it. She negotiated the price down to an unheard-of amount of $859,999 and move-in day was December 10, as Kim had paid cash for the home. That condo was worth one million, easy.

Chapter Twelve

"Wow thought Kim. Is Dr. Paul Smith tall, dark, and handsome or what? Where did that thought come from? It's too soon for any romance in my life. Still…he is rather scrumptious looking…and looking doesn't hurt anyone…those dark blue eyes are amazing Love at first sight? Only in the movies…or not…such a dream dish…"

Thanksgiving arrived right on schedule. Sadie and Alice did most of the cooking while Sarah, Kim, and Nancy made the side dishes and salads. Aaron and his fellow doctor and friend, Dr. Paul Smith, a neurosurgeon, were in the living room chatting and watching the end of the Macy's Thanksgiving Day Parade with Danny and Lisa. This year nine place settings decorated the dining table.

Liza and Rob texted Kim to wish her and Nancy, plus the Leawood's, Sadie, and Alice a Happy Thanksgiving. Liza had wanted to know how things were going, and said things were fine in Boston.

"Dinner is ready," announced Sadie. The roasted turkey came out perfect – it always did when Sadie cooked it. She also made homemade dinner rolls to go along with the turkey and gravy. Aaron would carve the bird like usual once the table was ready. It was a moment of pride and tradition for him to carve the bird after prayers said.

Alice created homemade cranberry sauce, sage dressing, and green bean casserole. Sarah's part was roasted sweet potatoes, ultra-fluffy mashed potatoes, and a corn casserole.

Nancy made her famous pumpkin, cherry, and pecan pies all baked to perfection, while Kim created a sinfully divine pumpkin cheesecake, a sure-fire favorite, and she laid out the table settings as her back was hurting. Coffee, tea, and apple cider rounded out the menu.

"It's time to eat everyone. Sit wherever you wish at the table. Aaron, you have the head spot with the turkey like always." Sarah rang a tiny bell and announced the meal was ready.

After finding seats, Aaron gave a prayer for all the blessings that had come their way during the year, and gratefulness that everyone was healthy and well, except for Kim's back problems.

Aaron carved the turkey while the others passed around side dishes, the women helping the children with their portions. The ambiance of being one big and happy family was in the air.

Chatter started and Aaron made sure the newcomers knew Dr. Paul Smith, was a neurosurgeon, at the same hospital he and Sarah worked at.

At one point Kim reached for a dinner roll and, "Ouch! My bad. I leant too far over, Nancy. Can you put an icy hot patch on me, please? I have a package in the kitchen." Both women left the table and Dr. Smith raised his eyebrow at Aaron and Sarah.

"I meant to mention this to you, Paul. Kim has lumbar pain and it's become worse over time. Think you have time to see her for a visit during this busy time of year?" Aaron queried Paul.

"Well, I'm off tomorrow, but I could make an exception and see Kim around 10am."

"What did you just say about me, Paul? Kim asked as the ladies sat back down to eat. She had the perfect excuse to look at his dark hair, chiseled face, and gorgeous dark blue eyes.

"Your lower back hurts, so I thought I could see you as a patient tomorrow at 10am at the hospital. It is my specialty, after all."

"Okay, I'll be there at 10am. I'm so tired of the pain. Thank you for taking me on as a new patient," Kim agreed as she smiled. "That's kind of you."

The rest of the meal and day went off without a hitch. Paul left for his home and everyone else stayed in the main house that evening.

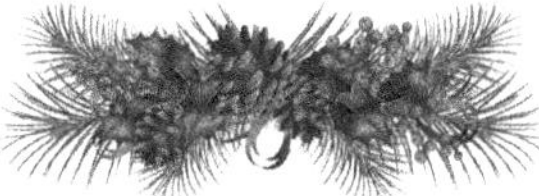

Kim arrived promptly just before 10am in the clinic area that Dr. Paul Smith worked at.

After greeting Kim, he led the way into an examination room, and gestured for her to sit in a padded chair. "Tell me about your back, Kim. Start at the beginning and tell me all the tests and treatment modalities you have undergone, please. Do you have any medical records with you? What symptoms do you currently have?"

"Well, Dr. Smith, it started with my scoliosis that went untreated since I was a child. As I got older, more problems popped up and they aren't slowing down, at all. I have pain all the time, and it shoots down both legs. Sometimes, I pray to Jesus to take away the worst of it when I can't get any relief from the bad painful times. My pain never goes away at all. I must change my position all the time, from sitting to standing and walking, to laying down on my side when I sleep. The pain wakes me up at night!" Kim exclaimed.

"The last time I had a moment without pain was two decades ago. At present, I take ibuprofen every 12 hours and I have a lumbar support brace on. The support brace has boning and wide, strong elastic bands, and it takes the edge off my pain part of the time."

"Call me Paul, please, as we are friends, but I'm still your doctor. Please continue with what you've tried. There's no need to repeat modalities that have failed you in the past," Paul replied as he documented on a portable laptop.

"I gave you my last MRI (Magnetic Resonance Imaging) report and the disc. Can you explain it to me so that I understand?

"Certainly," Paul responded. "First, the MRI was done with and without a special contrast so that greater visuality can be noted. You have bad scoliosis, as you know. Each vertebra is numbered as they go up. Look at this model of a spine."

Paul placed the plastic model within easy reach of Kim. "The spine is normally made up of 33 vertebrae. They are divided into five sections. The cervical section labeled C1 to C7, is connected to the base of the skull. Directly below the cervical vertebra is the thoracic section followed by the lumbar, sacrum, and coccyx sections. In your case, the area of concern starts at the S1 and goes up to the T12. Are you with me still?"

"Yes, I am so far," Kim said with a soft laugh. "I can see many vertebrae are involved and my scoliosis is in the same area. That curvature looks bad to me."

"The cause of your pain is complex, but I think I can explain it, so you understand. I will point out each area as we go. Your scoliosis is a left rotary type, and the curve is here." Paul pointed out on his laptop screen a picture of Kim's spine and used his hand to emphasize the part causing the pain.

"You have well-maintained lumbar lordosis that can cause you pain. Your back is arched and in the curve of the lumbar spine (just above the buttocks) is the problem area." Paul looked at Kim to see if she understood him.

"I can see that alright! I understand scoliosis and I see the different vertebrae. They don't look like the plastic model you showed me first." Kim sighed and wondered if there was any help for her issues. Her despondent emotions showed on her face.

"Let me finish explaining what is going on with your spine, okay? There are things we can try." Paul continued. "Don't give up yet. You have broad-based bulging discs from L3-L4 through L5-S1. That is the small cushion shapes between each vertebra, and it is one reason for your pain. You also have seven Tarlov cysts with the largest measuring 2.0 x 1.5 cm. Let me explain what those are, okay?"

"Yes, please and thank you. How did I ever get those and what are they exactly?" Kim asked. Her prior doctor in Boston never went into detail about her back and she wanted to learn all she could. "If you know what is going on, then that's half the battle, right?"

"Yes, it is, Kim. Tarlov cysts (also known as meningeal cysts or peri-neural cysts) are fluid-filled sacs (spinal fluid). Most are near the bottom of the spine (the sacrum). Your cysts are in the roots of the nerves. Causes are many such as shock or trauma to the spine, and exertion can cause spinal fluid in the cysts to build up. This, in turn, causes more pain."

"Okay. Can they be drained with a needle? Would that help me?" Kim was desperate to know what could be done.

"I will inform you of treatment options after I finish explaining your back problems, okay? I see how anxious you are. Can I get you a bottle of water? We still have territory to cover."

"Thank you for the water," Kim smiled after taking a long drink. "I was thirsty!"

"The next part is the cause for most of your pain. With the canal narrowing at L4-L5 you have nerve root impingement at both levels, the left greater and more severe than the right side, but both sides are affected." Paul quietly waited for Kim to reply.

"That's not good at all. Nerve impingement is not a good thing. My back has serious issues and I'm scared that nothing will help me with my pain." Kim finally spoke in a soft voice. A look of fear and hopelessness consumed her.

Kim looked fatigued and worn out. "Hope remains, Kim. Don't give up just yet. The next step is for you to tell me what was tried in the past to help decrease your pain." *I must help Kim…I must see a lot of her pain going away…I hurt to see Kim hurting…Kim in one extra fine woman…where did that idea come from? Love at first sight? Never…yet…maybe…*

"My doctor in Boston first tried steroid (for inflammation) injections, six of them, in that area of my back. It didn't work. Then he gave me six more steroid injections. They failed; steroids were not the answer for me. Boy do those injections hurt!" Kim exclaimed, and each time she had to have a driver, usually Nancy.

"My next step was Bupivacaine (pain medicine) injections, six of them around my nerves. It didn't work. I felt zero relief. But I had to have this process repeated for an adequate trial. Six more Bupiva-caine injections, and I had zero relief yet again." After a long sigh, Kim looked up at Paul and she knew her hopelessness showed in her eyes and on her face.

"Okay, Kim, I have that documented and I will send for your medical records in Boston, if you sign this release, please." He handed the sheet of paper and a pen to Kim, and she filled it out and gave both back to him. "What else did you try to help with your back pain?"

"I saw three different surgeons who won't touch me; they thought surgery was not an option for me. I also saw a renowned rheumatologist in Boston, and I tried different non-narcotic methods to see if they would help. Among them was Gabapentin and Cymbalta. None helped, some made me dizzy and unsteady, and one gave me terrible hand tremors." Kim added, "I've taken Flexeril (muscle relaxer) twice a day for about two decades," she exhaled slowly.

"The last thing I had done was high temperature ablation burning of three minutes each to six nerves, and it hurt like heck! Sadly, it failed, and my nerves took out their anger on me with even worse pain and put me in the ER. While there, the doctor looked at my ablation sites, saw how I changed position every other minute from lying on gurney, to bending over the head of the gurney and multiple positions throughout my visit. I received steroids IV (for inflammation) to help calm my angry nerves, two small doses of Fentanyl IV (for pain), and something else that I can't remember. Nothing else has been done," Kim added with a downcast appearance. "I'm out of options, aren't I?"

"No. I have an idea that may make your pain bearable." Paul reached for another plastic spine model and placed it in front of Kim. "Why don't you get up and stretch around a bit. Then sit back down and I'll tell, and show you, what I have in mind."

After a restroom and walking break, Kim sat back down in her chair and waited for Paul to come back into the room. *"Maybe there is hope for*

me, for my back, just maybe…Paul looks so handsome in his scrubs, so muscular, so hot…where did that come from??? Oh, those biceps are divine! I've fallen for this man. How does that happen in real life? Yet here I am, and that is how I feel…such an attraction to Paul."

Paul walked in and sat down. "I think that a Nerve Spinal Cord Stimulation Therapy Trial may help with your back pain. Look at this model in front of you. Wires go up both sides of your spine. The idea is the pulse generator would deliver electrical pulses directly to the spinal cord, thereby blocking pain signals from reaching the brain. I suggest a one-week trial if you are so inclined. Do you want to hear more, Kim?"

"Yes, Paul, I want to know more. I need to know what to expect to decide on doing this or not."

"Both the maker of the device representative, and my office would speak with you each day and tell you how to change the settings on the stimulating generator. After placement of the wires, I will see where each wire is as you will be on continuous fluoroscopy during the procedure, I would then place a large sterile dressing over the entire area, a big dressing with multiple layers and flexible tape. Finally, I would secure the pulse generator with flexible tape on the right side of your lower back." Paul explained.

"You can't take a bath or shower during the trial. The area must stay sterile and dry, no bacteria can enter the insertion site as that would infect your spinal fluid. You will have a remote control to adjust the settings as directed by device tech each time they call. You must have a driver on the day of placement, and you must not take any medicine that thins the blood for one week prior to placement. No aspirin, no ibuprofen, not even a baby aspirin."

Paul looked at me and stated, "You cannot do any bending or holding more than 10 pounds in your arms during the trial. Here are some handouts to look at and give me a call if you wish to try this, okay?"

"Thank you, Paul. I have a lot to think about. Maybe there is hope for me after all!" Kim replied as she stood up to leave.

"Before you leave, may I have your mobile number? I will have Aaron consult on your case."

"Sure." Kim handed her number to him, and he gave her a business card after he wrote his mobile on the back side of the card. "Thank you for taking the time to inform me of everything and I will think this over. Bye!" Kim smiled as she walked out the door. *Maybe, just maybe… hope is a good thing, and maybe, just maybe…this might work…romance…love… I bet he doesn't give all his patients his mobile number. WOW! I must be special to him. Or I'm reading more into this than there is…time will tell.*

Chapter Thirteen

*K*im thought about what Paul had said regarding her back and a possible nerve stimulator trial as she drove back to Aaron and Sarah's house. She'd pondered on the information he had given to her. Now she wanted to hear opinions from Aaron, Sarah, and Nancy. Aaron's especially, since he was an ER doctor and he consulted on neuro cases, after all.

After dinner that evening, everyone stayed in that Friday night. Sadie and Alice had gone back to their cottages for the night, and both children were in bed fast asleep.

"Is something on your mind, Kim? You've looked like you wanted to talk all evening." Nancy asked of her dear friend. "How is your back pain doing?"

"Oh. You always read me like a book, Nancy." Both Aaron and Sarah looked at Kim and all three awaited her answer. "My pain right now is 8/10. So, it could be worse, and this recliner helps me in the position I am, partly on my right side with this support pillow stuck firmly against my spine. Thank you for asking."

Looking directly at Aaron, Kim continued, "Paul thinks that a Spinal Cord Stimulation Therapy Trial might help me. I want your thoughts, Aaron. You know as much about neuro as Paul and I want your honest opinion."

"As you know, I consulted on your case, Kim, and I looked over your last MRI and treatments you have tried in the past. In all honesty, I think you have a 60/40 chance, in your favor, of a nerve stimulation trial helping your pain level to decrease. A five-day trial would be enough time to adequately measure changes in your pain level."

Sarah nodded her head in agreement as she leaned back on the sofa and into her husband's lap. "I'm with Aaron on this one."

Looking back and forth Nancy was lost. "What the heck does the spinal cord thing do? Is it even safe? Could it paralyze Kim?" Fear, concern, and worry plainly showed on her face.

Aaron explained the process to her in simple non-medical terms and Nancy nodded her understanding.

"Well, that gives you something to think about over the weekend, Kim. I'm pooped. My bed is calling to me. I think all three of you look tired. Good night." Nancy headed for the stairs and her bed.

Saturday morning arrived and Sadie had left fresh biscuits on the counter, and sausage gravy in the refrigerator for Kim and Nancy to reheat in the microwave. A fresh pot of coffee assailed their senses before they reached the kitchen. A note left on the counter informed them that the Leawood's had already left to do some shopping in town, Sadie was at her home working on Christmas crafts, and Alice's book club were to meet at 10am.

"We are on our own, Kim. I'll grab two mugs and plates with utensils, and you grab the sausage gravy to reheat in the microwave, okay?" Nancy asked, as she prepared the biscuits for the gravy. Once all was done, they took their food to the breakfast nook in the dining room and sat down to eat and chat.

Glancing out the window they saw two elk near some pines, both female. The elk reminded Kim of the elk in Evergreen, and women decided to take a drive up and into the Heart of Evergreen.

Before heading out, Kim took the time to text Liza and Rob. She let them know how things were going with Nancy and herself, and then asked if they had a nice Thanksgiving. They texted back that all was great in Boston, cold and snowy, but good.

Upon arriving in The Heart of Evergreen, Kim parked her Jeep in the Lake House Parking Lot. "What do you want to do first, Nancy?"

"I think a leisurely stroll around the lake would be a nice way to start. We would see more of the lake area as we go." Off they went, taking their time strolling around the lake.

Even in the daytime, the snow on the lake and snow laden pine trees were gorgeous. The walking path was completely clear for use.

Taking a deep breath in, Kim slowly exhaled. "I love this town, the lake, the scenery, and you, Nancy, my sister from two different parents! Just think, back in Boston, we would be freezing our butts off right now in the damp cold, but here, at over 7000 feet, the drier cold certainly isn't as cold."

"True," Nancy smiled. "However, they do have wet snow from time to time. I imagine that a more wet snow here would still be warmer than Boston's cold, damp, and frigid temperatures."

The lake path was clear and both women wore hiking boots. Scattered out on the snow-covered part of the lake, at least a dozen small tents for ice fishing were noted.

"I read that this lake freezes over each winter, by December 1, and ice fishing and skating take over the lake. There's no fee to fish the lake, if you have a fishing license, and parking is free." Kim informed Nancy as they continued to stroll. "Oh, and Sarah and her family come up to ice skate as often as they can."

"Oh look, a sign over there," Nancy spoke up. "Let's read it."

The signage regarded ice fishing and ice skating. Both read that safe ice should be your number one consideration when ice fishing. A minimum of three to four inches of solid ice is the general rule for safety. Ice thickness, however, is not uniform on any body of water. Evidently, the ice fisherpersons had to know the depth before setting up.

As they rounded the southeast area of the lake, they stopped to take a rest. Both had exercised in the past but being above 7000 feet would take them time to acclimate. "Well, I've got my brace on with all the boning in it, and the support, but my back needs a short break, too."

"Of course, Kim. Take a good rest. Your health comes first, and it is always health and people first. You know that. Like I've said before, you're my sister. Not by blood, but family is who you choose to include in one's family. I chose you a long time ago. We chose each other. We'll always be family, no matter what," as the women high fived each other with their gloved hands.

Along the south side of the lake many houses were seen, some bigger, some smaller, but everyone they came across on the walking path gave a friendly smile and said hello. Not to be outdone, the women did the same. "I feel so welcome here," Kim smiled as she looked over to Nancy who smiled back.

"Stop," Nancy spoke quietly. Kim looked in the direction Nancy pointed and saw two majestic bull elk with huge antlers.

They stopped and simply watched the elk from a safe distance. "This is so awesome," Kim whispered, then she laughed because whispering wasn't necessary.

After watching the elk do what they did, both ladies grabbed their mobiles and took some photos. Kim was a true "shutterbug" and Nancy was well on her way to becoming one, too.

As the elk moved away, the ladies resumed their walk along the lake path while keeping a safe distance from the elk.

'I'm so glad and excited to know that The Heart of Evergreen is our new home." Nancy sighed. A fresh start was what the doctor ordered, and this was true "thing" for them. What had once been a dream of living in Colorado, had become reality and a fresh new start in their lives.

Closer to the Lake House, snow had been pushed off the ice, leaving small embankments surrounding the cleared ice. "Would you look at that. Those people aren't just skating, they are playing a game of hockey!" Kim exclaimed.

Finally, they reached Kim's Jeep and got inside. Smiling at each other, both realized how much they had fallen in love with the area.

"Let's find a place for a late lunch, Kim. We could go to one of those quaint shops on 74 and simply pick one at random to eat."

They ended up at Heart of Evergreen Bistro, for sustenance. Parking was at a premium. The area bubbled over with people coming and going, and a vibe of tangible excitement assailed their senses. From the outside, the atmosphere was palpable and full of energy. Between the indoor and outdoor Christmas décor surrounding them and the lights, came a sense of being home, in the right place, and at the right time. God had directed them home.

The Heart of Evergreen Bistro was quaint in appearance and to the west of it was a crafts store and to the east was an art gallery. In the window was a For Sale sign. Kim knew she would be checking that gallery out after they ate lunch.

Seated at a booth near a window that overlooked the lake, they decided to order the house soup of the day, a delicious sounding potato and leek soup, with crusty bread and a dip. Nancy decided to have hot cocoa and Kim chose iced tea with a lemon slice.

While they ate the soup, they overheard a couple talking in the booth behind Kim. They weren't eavesdropping intentionally; they simply overheard the couple talking about the art gallery next door closing.

Nancy and Kim looked each other in the eye. Smiling, Kim decided she was going to ask the couple about the shop, as she was interested in buying it, and having a gallery in Evergreen was on her to do list, after all. After eating their lunch faster than usual, Kim stood up and Nancy followed her to the next booth.

"Excuse me, please. I'm sorry but I overheard you mention the gallery next door was closing. Do you know the owner? I'm interested in purchasing the gallery and any information would be greatly appreciated," Kim said as she smiled down at the older couple. "I'm an artist and I have many gallery pieces headed this way as I closed my gallery in Boston and moved to Evergreen recently."

"Welcome to Evergreen. I'm Fred Browning and this is my wife, Barbara."

"Please call me Barb," replied Mrs. Browning. "Have a seat in our booth, there's plenty of room."

In unison, Kim and Nancy said thank you and sat down with the older couple.

"Sure, we can discuss the gallery as we own it," Barb spoke up first. "We love the gallery dearly, but the time has come to sell it. Our daughter, Kristin, and her husband, Bob, live in the Coral Gables area of Miami."

"Kristin needs help, more than Bob can provide, and their three children are quite busy with school and extracurriculars." Fred sighed. "It's not easy selling our art gallery, but we must."

Barb took over and added, "Our daughter is in the early process of fighting aggressive breast cancer. Her battle is wicked, and Bob has difficulty working and fitting in cancer treatments, doctor visits, lab draws, the children, school events, cooking, and cleaning."

"They have friends to help out, but they need full time help," Bob explained. "Kristen is in week three of her fight with cancer and she has zero energy. Bob can't do it all and they could hire a woman to help, but we need to be in Coral Gables. Our daughter and her family need us, and we need them."

"Exactly! It is the only right thing to do. Family comes first," Barb stated, "and their home is large. We'd move into their home and help where and when needed."

"I'm so sorry to hear this about Kristen," Kim looked at Fred and Barb. She could tell that the past three weeks had taken a toll on them as well. Worry was written all over their faces.

"Cancer battles are always hard," replied Nancy. It's hard on everyone in the family. Your son-in-law must be absolutely exhausted between work, the medical trips, the children, and home care needed for all five of them."

"How about we show you the gallery now?" Barb inquired.

"Great!" Kim was enthused about the gallery, yet sad that the couple had to leave the place they loved and Kristin having a tough fight with cancer.

The meal checks settled, all four headed out the door.

Chapter Fourteen

The Swiss chalet and river stone style façade of the two-floor, steep-pitched, and gabled roof of the gallery was decorated for Christmas and looked amazing.

"Evergreen receives snow, and the pitch and gable of the roof allows for heavy or light snow accumulation to slide off and down to the ground." Fred explained as he pointed to the roof.

He unlocked the front door to the gallery and flipped the sign to "open" as the women walked on in. The open floor concept allowed for ample wall space for having art, and a ginormous glass-encased, lit up center island showcased carved wood and metal artworks.

"As you can see there are different gallery pieces hanging on the walls, sitting on shelves, and under glass are the ones that are a little smaller and pricier, so they are locked up under the glass." Barb offered as she showed Kim and Nancy the back side and how the key lock system worked.

"Honestly, when the shop is busier near the holidays, spring break, and throughout the summer, it can be quite hectic. If a person truly wants to purchase a piece, they will wait until we are done with the customer preceding them, and nothing gets stolen. Look at some of the gold, silver, and bronze pieces and you will understand this locking glass display case is a must for the gallery."

Barb continued, "Some of the artworks hanging on the walls are pricier than others but they are larger and it's not as easy to walk out," Fred replied. "Not much, if any, crime happens here in the Heart of Evergreen, but best practice is best practice."

Essentially, the gallery would be sold "as is" with the remaining artworks on display. Some were created by Fred and Barb, and other pieces were commissioned by local artists. Kim would "inherit" the arrangement. Half of the wall space was empty so there was room for her to add some of her own works.

The modern, locked when-not-in-use cash register sat on a small attached-to-the-wall island, and access was difficult due to a locked wooden gate; hence customers couldn't get in without someone seeing it happen.

Down a small hallway were two bathrooms, one for men and one for women and both were family oriented. The back room was well lit like the main gallery, and one area was for gift wrapping small and large pieces for any occasion. The easels would stay, and the paints and brushes would go to Florida.

The upstairs included the gabled roof with a steep pitch, and the space was used mostly for storage. "What do you think, Kim? Will this gallery work for you?" Fred asked. "Take your time and think it over." He handed Kim his business card.

"I do love the look and layout of the gallery, and this is a prime spot. Thank you for your card, but I can tell you right now I love this shop. It "speaks" to my heart, and I see this as a great opportunity. Nancy is my Administrative Assistant, and we both would fit right in." Kim stated as she looked around the main showroom. "Let's talk price."

After tossing numbers back and forth a few times, Kim and the current owners settled on a purchase price. Barb called their realtor, who was in town, and she drove over to the gallery.

The realtor said that it would be 30 days before she could close and take ownership of the gallery and Kim replied that she would pay in cash if she could have it sooner. Details were worked out, and paperwork drawn up on the realtor's laptop. Electronic signatures completed, and the paperwork printed via the printer near the cash register.

Since purchasing in cash, Kim could take ownership on December 10 – the same day she was to move into her condo! Since it was furnished, both women could sleep their first night in Evergreen at her new condo.

Kim and Nancy were elated! Life was going in their favor, and both felt blessed by Jesus for being in the right place at the right time today. It was meant to be.

Kim figured that she could have boxes unloaded at her new condo, and then the paintings, art works, paints, and all the supplies could take up the rest of the day at the gallery, and she would pay the movers extra to hang paintings where she wanted them.

This meant that they had only 12 days until December 10. Talk about a whirlwind of excitement for the women and the current owners. This gave Fred and Barb time to pack up what they were keeping from the gallery and pack up their personal belongings at home. All that remained was for Nancy to find a home of her own.

The realtor asked Fred and Barb if anyone was interested in purchasing the house they had for sale. Nancy overheard the question and answer, so she casually walked up and said, "Have you sold your home yet? I'm looking for home in Evergreen, too."

Startled, Barb said they had not sold their house yet, and hoped to sell it fully furnished soon. *And they were off to see the house…*

Chapter Fifteen

*B*arb stayed at the gallery while Fred followed the realtor and Kim followed Fred up 74 west, past the turnoff for Kim's new condo, and soon, they pulled into the driveway of two floor, three bed and three bath log and river rock home.

The realtor went right into realtor mode starting with the wrap-around porch with fairy lights strung throughout and wooden outdoor furniture graced the porch. The heavily treed home screamed welcome.

From the main entrance of the home, a lovely wood accented entry-way led into a large, yet cozy, main living area with exposed beams.

A large dark leather wrap-around sofa, loveseat, and three matching recliners were grouped around a rounded coffee table topped with natural wood and three side matching side tables.

In front of the seating area was a large river rock fireplace and above it hung a large screen 75-inch flat screen television. Antler ceiling lights hung from above. Plenty of windows allowed natural light to filter inside.

Adjacent to the main living area was a dining room that had a six-seat, carved walnut dining table topped with candles and Christmas décor. Additional antler ceiling lights hung above the table and a matching carved walnut sideboard held more Christmas décor. The room practically screamed out for those who entered to sit down, get cozy, and that dinner would arrive in short order. A gas fireplace of river rock was decorated with tall candles and fake greenery.

Through an arched wooden doorway was a fully equipped gourmet kitchen with wooden cupboards and all stainless-steel appliances. Granite countertops, an additional wine fridge, and a breakfast bar area for four completed the open design. Track lighting gave off a warm glow, and the pantry was large enough to feed a platoon of soldiers. Well, not really, but the size was quite generous.

Off the kitchen was a laundry and mud room and a back entrance led straight into the attached two car garage.

Back inside, the guest bathroom was located off the main living area down a short hallway. Next to it was a linen closet and across from the guest bathroom was the master bedroom.

The ensuite master bedroom held a dark brown, carved walnut queen size bed and dark brown walnut furniture along with one walk-in closet. The bathroom included a walk-in shower and a jacuzzi. *How utterly nice, Nancy thought... I've found my new dream home and I'm ready to start my new life afresh... If the price is right...*

Both Nancy and Kim were impressed and smiled at each other as they were led back into the main living area and over to a carved wooden spiral stair that led directly into a reading nook/library, on a landing that overlooked the main living space.

Two steps up were a hallway with a full bath and two guest bedrooms. Both were fitted with full bed sets and matching furniture. Antler lights hung above the bed in one bedroom while a ceiling fan with lights hung in the other.

Back in the dining room, they sat down to discuss the purchase price. Fred reminded the realtor that all furniture was included except for the master bed itself. That bed was going to Florida with him and Barb as it had been custom made for them, the mattress set was brand new, and it had taken them a long time to find the right comfort bed set perfect for them and their needs.

Fifteen minutes later, Nancy declared the home was going to be hers, and that it would be a cash sale. The details were worked out, and the realtor brought out her laptop once again and drew up the sales contract. Electronic signatures were completed, and the paperwork was printed. Fred and Barb had 30 days to get their belongings packed and the bed shipped to Florida.

What a day, indeed! If I hadn't seen and heard today with my own eyes and ears, never would I have believed this happened... Not... At... All...

Chapter Sixteen

$\mathcal{A}$aron opened the door as Kim and Nancy stepped onto the front porch deck. "Come inside and get warm. You two have been gone all day long."

"Yeah, what's up with you two. I can see it written on your faces." Sarah commented. "Spill the beans now. You two did something cool so tell us. I know that look on your face, Kim."

Sadie went to make a pot of coffee, sandwiches, and hot cocoa for the children as the doorbell rang.

"Hold that thought for a minute," Aaron replied as he answered the front door and welcomed Paul inside. Everyone got comfortable and situated near the fireplace with their drinks and refreshments Sadie had made. Danny and Lisa had hot cocoa near the fire.

"Kim and Nancy were up to something today and we were asking for them to spill the beans," Sarah laughed. "I know something big happened. Look at their faces!"

"Oh," Paul raised an eyebrow. "Do tell." All eyes went straight to Kim and Nancy's faces.

"Really, there isn't much to tell," Kim giggled which caused Nancy to laugh out loud.

"Truly, I have no beans to spill," then Kim cracked up laughing hard. "All we did was take a drive to Evergreen. It's so amazing there. Still, no beans to spill," as she laughed out loud once again with Nancy joining her, in the mood of the moment.

Who would have thought that both women would be laughing with their friends in Colorado after what they'd endured in Boston only a few weeks earlier.

"I know you better, Kim," Sarah replied with narrowed eyes, "and both of you laughing means you BOTH did something. So, spill it now, right now!"

"Okay, the gig is up. I drove us up to Evergreen in my Jeep." Kim snickered. "Once there, I parked in the parking lot at the Lake House."

Nancy giggled and all eyes went straight to her. "I give up. We took a leisurely stroll around the lake."

All eyes went right to Kim when Paul asked, "Really, Kim? You walked around the lake? How does your back feel?"

"My back is okay, Paul. My pain is 8/10 but the day was rather a busy one. Honest. We didn't walk fast like the other walkers out on the path, and we took rest stops. We stopped and read the signage about the lake rules and took a few photos of the ice fishing tents out on the snow." Kim smiled, recalling the walk as she stretched to calm down the pain she felt in her back.

Nancy fetched an icy hot patch and placed it on Kim's back, before sitting back down. "Thanks a lot," Kim smiled at her friend and cohort of the day.

"And when we turned the corner of the southeast part, we took another break," Nancy added. "But something cool did happen as we saw a couple of bull elk nuzzling in the snow. We let them guide us as to how we walked. As the elk moved off, we stayed on the path never getting too close. We must have taken a thousand mobile pictures!"

"Elk are cool!" Danny blurted out. "Sorry. I was excited." Lisa was all ears at the mention of the elk, too.

"That's true! The elk were majestic," Kim agreed before falling into giggles yet again.

"Aunt Kim!" Danny grinned, "You are funny today. So is Nancy."

After giving Danny a wink, Sarah looked Kim in the eye, "You had best spill the rest of the beans right now. I can read you like a book and I want to know now. More than a walk and a few elk happened."

"We are spilling it, Sarah. That is what happened. Near the Lake House, we saw how the snow was removed from the ice and formed embankments around the ice. Guys were out on the ice playing hockey. Then we got inside my Jeep and decided to get a cup of coffee and sustenance at one of the bistros."

Nancy took over then. "We spotted the Heart of Evergreen Bistro, pulled in, and parked. We walked toward the bistro and Kim noticed a For Sale sign in the art gallery next door to the bistro. We also saw a sign, in the window of the front door, that stated the shop would reopen in about 45 minutes."

Smiling, Nancy continued, "At the bistro, we sat at a window that looked out upon the lake. The house soup of the day, was a divinely and delicious potato and leek soup, with crusty bread, a dip, and drinks."

Kim giggled as she whispered, "We overheard the couple in the next booth chatting. Honest! It was honestly a simple overhearing of the voices. But then we heard mention of the art gallery and we *intentionally* listened in on the conversation." Kim laughed.

"I've overheard bits and pieces of conversations inside dining establishments in the past, in different places, but this time, we both *intentionally* listened as we ate our soup fast." Now Kim and Nancy were both laughing again.

"You see, we didn't want the couple to leave just yet," Nancy added. "We were on a mission to find out more about the quaint gallery."

"Then what happened?" Aaron asked as both women erupted in a fit of giggles once again.

The children giggled with them because they were happy for Kim and Nancy.

"I'll tell you, but you won't believe it," Kim replied. "We got up and walked over to the booth next to us, and introduced ourselves to the older couple, Fred, and Barbara Browning. Well, I apologized that we had overheard the word 'gallery' in their conversation about the gallery."

"Kim did apologize, yes, indeed," added Nancy. Smiling at Kim, she told her to continue the tale of day.

"They turned out to be the gallery owners. Long story short, they had to sell the art gallery, as their daughter recently started a huge battle with aggressive breast cancer, and they planned to move to Florida and help her entire family. Of course, we spoke of how sad we were for the family." Kim became quiet and lost in thought.

"That is a sad situation but…. More happened. The suspense is killing me. I know you did more than talk with the older couple. I can read it on your face, Kim. You can't hide anything from me, remember? Did you go look at it?" Sarah demanded the truth while she smiled.

Kim informed everyone that the gallery owners didn't want to sell, but their daughter, her husband, and their three children had needs that ran her husband ragged. It was a bad situation for the entire family.

"Cancer is hard all around, especially when your own child has it, no matter the age of your child, but especially the sweet children." Sarah spoke up as memories washed over and through her of her youngest son fighting a huge cancer battle of his own, before passing away from his ordeal, a full year-long ordeal.

"I'm sorry, Sarah. I didn't mean to make you sad." Kim gave her friend a hug.

"It's okay. The memories keep my son from being forgotten. I'm so sorry to hear this about their daughter. If I had a magic wand, and I wish I did, cancer would be the first thing I'd make disappear!"

"Cancer battles are always hard," replied Nancy as she looked at Sarah with compassion. "It's hard on everyone in the family. There are so many trips to doctors, labs, treatments, the kids' activities, school, working, grocery shopping, cooking, the list is endless. The needs of the many are too much for one parent alone. Then Kim told them she was looking for a gallery to purchase."

"Wait… What?" Paul was confused. "What did you do? I didn't realize that you are an artist, Kim. You must be quite talented if you are looking for a gallery to purchase." Both women giggled back at Paul.

"I am, Paul. I owned my own gallery in Boston, and I'll tell you more about it another time. Kim wants to hear all the beans so… Anyway, Fred and Barb showed us the gallery. I fell in love with the Swiss chalet and river stone style façade of the two-floor, steep-pitched, and gabled gallery roof." The place had felt like it had her name written all over it.

"The Christmas lights and décor looked amazing. I decided to purchase it and Fred called his realtor who came over to the gallery. A price was settled upon and get this! Since I paid cash for it, I get to take over ownership on December 10 – the same day I take over ownership of my new condo!"

"Wow, Kim! I'm so happy for you!" Sarah gushed. "That explains all the giggles and the looks on your faces."

That comment brought forth peals of laughter from Kim and Nancy, again!

Looking closely at both women, Aaron remarked that they must have had more excitement that needed to be spilled.

Sarah agreed with her husband and ordered the women, in a nice way to, "Start talking and don't stop until all the beans are out. And I do mean *all* the beans!"

"The realtor asked Fred and Barb if anyone was interested in the mountain home they were selling." Kim laughed again, and it felt great to be able to laugh once more, to have a life again, and not one of living in fear. That one single twenty-four period back in Boston was receding from her mind.

"So, we drove west on 74 past Kim's condo and pulled into the driveway of a two floor, three bed, and three bath, log and river rock home." Nancy showed everyone a few pictures on her mobile of the home they'd been shown.

"Did you buy it?" Sarah simply had to know, and Aaron and Paul nodded in agreement.

Looking at their hosts, Nancy grinned, "As a matter of fact, I did just that! It's my dream home and I take possession in 30 days!"

Aaron, Sarah, and Paul all had their jaws hanging open in shock.

"You two are putting us on," Paul remarked. "Great joke and suspense," he laughed. "How could all of that happen in one single day? No way!"

After another round of laughter along with a brief discussion that proved their adventure that day, congratulations were given to Kim and Nancy.

"This calls for champagne." Nancy got up to grab a bag, "I have a bottle with me that I picked up when we finally left Evergreen.

Aaron went to get glasses and champagne was poured for all.

"Aaron and I don't drink often, but this is a celebration," Sarah replied. "Now for a toast. Kim, congratulations on finding the perfect gallery you wanted. Nancy, we are all thrilled you found a new home. Cheers!" Soft clinks of the glasses and everyone took a sip of champagne.

Paul gave Kim a warm smile as he noticed her eyes were shining with happiness.

Kim didn't miss the look Paul gave her as his eyes stayed on her for a long time; the warmth, the honesty, the drown-me-in-your-eyes look.

What was hopeless four short weeks ago had turned into a perfect day with a perfect ending with friends celebrating the events.

Chapter Seventeen

Sunday started out with a lovely breakfast, after which everyone bundled up for church, the church that the Leawood's attended, Light of the World Catholic Church located west of their home in Lakewood. Since Sadie and Alice also went to the same church, two vehicles were needed to shuffle everyone there.

After services were over, they drove back home. Once there Sadie checked on the pork roast cooking in the roaster, and she saw it was done to perfection. Sarah and Nancy set the table as Kim supervised both children in washing their hands.

Aaron declared the roast was amazing and both children nodded in agreement. The meal included roasted potatoes and asparagus tips with a cherry pie (Danny's favorite) for dessert.

The clean-up went fast and soon everyone gathered near the fire. Sadie went to her house as she was still making Christmas gifts and Alice sat down in a corner recliner with the current book she was reading.

Danny and Lisa dragged Aunt Kim into the playroom. They wanted to play Chinese checkers and the kids won each time.

The lazy Sunday afternoon flew by too fast. When the doorbell rang, Aaron answered it and invited Paul inside.

Kim's eyes met Paul's and he spoke up rather fast, "I know you didn't expect to see me, but I need to talk with Kim. We'll go to the dining room for privacy."

At the cozy breakfast/reading nook, they sat down. *Such dreamy eyes, Kim sighed...*

Then she realized Paul was in 'doctor' mode and fear came over her.

"What is wrong?" Kim asked with alarm on her face. "I need you to tell me now."

"Nothing is wrong, Kim. I wanted to tell you in person that I have a cancellation tomorrow morning. My staff and I have a two-hour time slot, and, if you choose to do so, I can place the trial nerve stimulator in your back, if you want to try it, no pressure, no rush at all."

Paul's intensely warm eyes confirmed that he believed the trial had a chance of success and that was what she needed.

"I'm ready, Paul. I trust you, and I see that trust in your eyes." Their hands found each other, and they held hands for a short while, saying nothing, only looking into each other's eyes.

I've fallen in love with this man, even though I've barely known him for long... So easy to talk with, honest, caring, and more…or is it his doctor persona and bedside manner that I love? No… it is the man sitting next to me…I want to kiss him…do more with him…such a divine man…

Kim's inner and outer beauty hit me like a ton of bricks! I've never felt anything like this with other women…Could she be 'the one'? Have I gone and lost my mind? So beautiful, thoughtful, caring, brave, funny, and honest…I'd kiss her, but she might run away from me…Oh, how I want to devour those pink lips!!! What did I get myself into?

Chapter Eighteen

Monday morning arrived and following Dr. Paul's orders, Kim took a special shower with antibacterial soap, dressed in pajama pants, a T-shirt, and had a light breakfast of toast and coffee with Nancy in the breakfast nook. Nancy would be her driver after the procedure this morning.

Aaron and Sarah had left for work, the children were in school, and Alice was helping Sadie with the grocery list for the week. They would go grocery shopping after Kim and Nancy had left, just in case either one needed one of them.

Kim was nervous and Nancy tried to assuage her nervousness and she did just that! Nancy was laughing, then she popped out with, "You wanted Dr. Paul to get you horizontal and now he will. Just not in the sexual way you dream of, girlfriend! I know you and that look. You DO dream of you and Paul horizontal!!!"

Both women cracked up with laughter and Kim blushed an embarrassing shade of red. "Just for that, you can drive me to the clinic for my procedure as well as drive me back here afterwards!" More loud peals of laughter caught the attention of Alice and Sadie.

Upon entering the dining room, Alice and Sadie peered at the women for a bit, not speaking. That brought on more another round of laughter. Alice smiled, then told them that they had best get a move on to the clinic as it was time for them to leave.

"Yes, Mom," replied Kim as they left the breakfast nook in giggles.

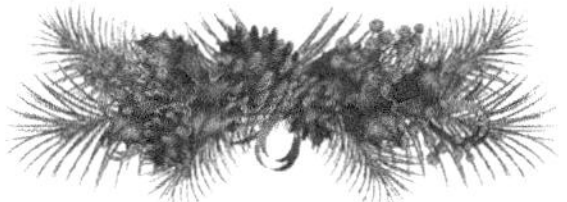

Nancy pulled the Jeep into a nearby parking spot that had just been vacated near the front door of the clinic. Together they walked inside, and Kim registered her arrival at the front desk before she sat down with Nancy to wait.

Ten minutes later, Kim's name was called and both women followed the nurse into a pre-procedure room. "My name is Erin and I'm your nurse this morning. Please have a seat in this chair, Kim. Who do you have with you?" Erin asked as she brought medical supplies over to Kim.

"This is Nancy. She's my driver today," Kim smiled, feeling relaxed with her nurse.

"Nancy, I'll have you sit in the other chair, and we'll get this process started," Erin nodded at Nancy before turning back to Kim.

She looked at Kim and asked for her full name and date of birth, which Kim complied with.

"Do you have any allergies, Kim?

"No, none yet. I think we are good on that score." Kim smiled back at Erin as she documented in the computer medical record.

"Now, I'm going to put an electronic vital sign recorder on your arm. Which arm do you prefer?"

"Please use my left arm, thanks for asking," Kim replied, and she looked over at Nancy, who appeared relaxed and without a care in the world.

"Great! This little monitor goes on the finger of your right hand so that I can obtain a baseline oxygen saturation on you. 97 percent is normal." Erin removed the blood pressure cuff and oximeter.

"Now we need to go over the medications you currently take." Erin looked at Kim and she replied that she took a muscle relaxer twice a day and gave the nurse the name of the medicine and her dosage.

Erin had inserted an IV in Kim's right hand when Dr. Paul came into the pre-procedure room. *Kim was beautiful...Of the ravishing kind...those pink lips... Get your mind out of the gutter and back to being a professional, Paul!*

He informed Kim that everything was in place, and the tech, Todd, from the company that made the device, would be present throughout.

Kim sighed, again. *Dr. Paul had a perfect butt, nice and snug, in his scrubs as Kim watched him leave the room…why does he fill out his scrubs so well…and look at those unbelievable biceps! Why is romance running around in my head? I haven't been a widow that long, but then Steve did turn out to be an assassin, so that killed my love for him, fast!*

"Nancy, you can now go back to the waiting room," Erin requested as she administered a low dose of Versed to help Kim relax, and one gram of an IV antibiotic before grabbing the maintenance bag of normal saline and walking Kim into the procedure room.

Once there, Kim was instructed to lay down on the table prone (stomach) with her head positioned in the head well at the head of the surgical table.

Once her head was in place, Kim took both hands and reached over the sides and brought them both together in a silent prayer. She held this position for most of the procedure.

Everything was done in an orderly fashion and the staff were in sync.

Erin checked Kim's IV to make sure it was good, and then she donned a lead apron. Erin was the circulating nurse, and she monitored the IV, IV fluids, EKG, vital signs, and Kim's well-being.

Erin also placed a special nasal device in Kim's left nares (nose) that registered what her oxygen saturations were, as it was more accurate than a finger pulse oximeter. Electronic vital signs were taken every 10 minutes and Kim's IV fluid was on a slow drip.

With the EKG in place once more, the staff could see how the telemetry was reading Kim's heart for potential problems.

Kim reminded the nurse that her skin disliked most adhesives and that she would remove the leads herself when all was done. Staff could have the wires, but not the pads.

Thus far, the Versed had not helped Kim relax. She hoped it would soon.

After everyone was masked up, other procedure staff raised Kim's T-shirt to her armpits and lowered her pajama pants to halfway down her hips. Then Kim's back was scrubbed with Chloraprep, a strong antiseptic, twice.

Dr. Paul dropped a large surgical drape upon Kim's back with each end rolled up toward her neck, the other down her legs. It was finally time to begin.

Dr. Paul told Kim, "I'm going to inject lidocaine into your lower back in two areas. Try to relax. You will be fine."

"I feel the lidocaine burning," Kim replied. She'd never liked the burn of lidocaine in the past, but Kim figured the lidocaine was nothing compared to what was next.

Erin checked Kim's IV and her vital signs again, and she informed Kim what her saturations and blood pressure reading was. This helped Kim to be less anxious, and she thanked Erin for telling her.

Erin was kind, a good nurse, and Kim was appreciative of the care and empathy given to her.

"The lidocaine has now numbed your back where I injected it, Kim. The procedure will commence. Are you okay?" Dr. Paul enquired.

"I still don't feel the Versed helping me and I wish I did feel it." Kim stated in a matter-of-fact tone. She was bummed with anxiety, but she trusted Dr. Paul.

"I'm going to insert the first wire now. It will be threaded up the right side of your spine, through your nerves to the area where the tip is to rest. The fluoroscopy shows how the threading of the wire goes. I need you to tell me if you have sudden numbness in your leg."

"It hurts bad," Kim cried out as the wire grazed a vertebra halfway up. Erin asked her to take several deep breaths in and out.

"It's going to hurt, Kim. I'm threading this wire through your nerves and up your spine. Please do what Erin asked you to do. Take some slow and deep breaths in and out," Dr. Paul encouraged her.

Five minutes or so later Dr. Paul announced that the first wire was in place and secured. "Okay, Kim. That's one wire down and one more to go. Are you hanging in, okay?"

"I'm still here on the table. I haven't run off yet," Kim grumbled out, totally not a fan that her nerves were on edge, in heightened awareness, and the nerves informed Kim how much they didn't appreciate what Dr. Paul had placed through them.

"What are my vital signs and oximeter reading?" Kim asked to no one specific as all she could see face down was her hands, her IV site and tubing, and the floor.

Erin told Kim her blood pressure and oxygen concentration numbers and Kim was relieved to know they were in the normal range. She'd thought her blood pressure would be sky high right now. Maybe the Versed was helping a bit.

"It's time for the second wire. I'm threading it up the left side of your spine doing the same procedure as I did to your right side. If you feel a sharp numbness or anything unusual, speak up right away." Dr. Paul instructed Kim.

"Part way up, Kim. You are doing great. The curve of your spine is tighter on the curvature inside so it will take a bit longer. Can you move your feet, Kim? I need to see both feet move."

Kim moved both feet and said, "Yes, I can move both of my feet. My left leg feels totally numb, but, since I can move my left foot I'm doing okay, right?

"Correct, Kim. Try to relax as I thread the wire the rest of the way up. Take some deep breaths in and out and tell me when you are ready for me to continue." Dr. Paul instructed Kim in a calm voice.

I can do this...yes, I can...I can do this... Jesus, help me to help my back relax so the wire is placed exactly where it needs to be placed...please take the edge off my pain...all glory and honor to You, Lord...Amen...Think of the Lord, Kim, and keep praying...He has helped me every single time in the past...He has saved me!

"You can continue," Kim told Dr. Paul. *Jesus helped Kim once again... He is so good...with Jesus I can get through and do anything...*

Then Dr. Paul inserted the wire all the way up to where the tip needed to be. Once the second wire was in place, he informed Kim that it was in perfect placement.

"That's a huge relief." Kim sighed loudly; glad the wires were both in the correct placement.

"Now I will put a sterile dressing over the insertion site, up your back, and to both sides of your back. I'm covering a large area, even though the insertion site is quite small." Dr. Paul informed Kim as he dressed her insertion site.

The dressing was done in multiple layers. The device that triggered the nerves was placed near the right lower part of her back and secured with surgical tape.

"It's time to turn the device on with the remote and set your basic initial settings for the device. Tell me what you feel, Kim."

"I feel tingles in my spine, but no pain relief," she moaned.

"You won't feel pain relief at this time, Kim. You will be able to better judge relief tomorrow and in the next five days. You did great!" Dr. Paul encouraged Kim, and he instructed the staff to finish up as he left the surgical procedure room to document what he had done to Kim's back.

After doctor Dr. Paul left, Erin informed Kim that staff would remove the surgical drape, pull her T-shirt down over the dressing, and pull her pajama pants back into position.

"I'm going to remove the probe in your nose and stop the IV fluids." Erin instructed Kim as the staff were busy doing post procedure best practice work.

"Can you stand up?" Erin asked. "I can help you."

"No. Stop please. I know my back and I must get off the table my way. Is that a problem?"

"It's not a problem at all. I will be right next to you if you need help." Erin took a stand at Kim's side.

Kim slowly moved both legs over the left side of the surgical table and used her arms to push up her upper body. Then she stopped and told Erin to give her a minute before she stood.

Once upright and vertical, Erin held Kim's right arm as she slipped her feet into her soft leather slip on shoes. "Are you dizzy, Kim?

"No, I'm not dizzy. You can have these leads now." Kim handed the wires over to a staff person after taking them off. Another staff person held Kim's left arm and they walked her back into the pre procedure room and had Kim sit down in the chair.

Nancy was allowed to come back in, and she smiled at Kim. Nancy believed Kim was a super trooper. The device tech, Todd, followed Nancy into the room.

Erin and Todd went over directions on how to turn the handheld remote on and off.

Kim was instructed in how to use the remote and that the remote could only be turned on when he called each day. Todd showed Kim the settings and how they worked.

The plan was for Todd to call Kim every day at 10 am, and adjustments would be made over the phone after assessing where Kim's pain level was at.

Kim was reminded that the placement of the stimulator electrodes would decrease her pain level by blocking the pain signal from below in her lower back from reaching her brain.

She was reminded to not get the dressing wet, no bath, no shower, no jacuzzi, and she could have Nancy wash her legs since Kim was not allowed to bend over that far. No bending, no driving, and no lifting anything over eight pounds.

Kim could use antibacterial soap and water from a basin or special, disposable bath wipes. Kim was glad she had bought several packages of bath wipes, especially since they could be warmed up in the microwave.

"I'm going to take your IV out now. Do you want Coban to hold the IV site dressing in place?"

"Yes, Erin, that would be great." Afterwards, Kim gently removed the telemetry pads from her skin. The pads had left large red areas but no skin breakdown.

Erin then informed Kim that she could now leave with Nancy as her driver.

"Thank you for helping me,' Kim responded and with Nancy holding on to her left arm, the women left the building for home.

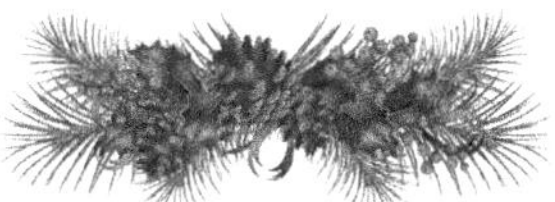

Once back at the Leawood home, Nancy helped Kim inside and to a recliner. Kim was steady in her step and balance, so she was okay to walk and move around on her own now.

"I pray this works, Nancy. My back hurts so bad and its way past time for me to have some relief. I pray tomorrow is a better day.

Soon after, Aaron, Sarah, and both children arrived home and they asked Kim how she was doing. Aaron said it was normal for her pain to be elevated post procedure and took a quick peek at her dressing site.

Sarah told Kim she would have Sadie make a sandwich, a couple cookies, and iced tea for her to eat before she went upstairs to her room. The evening was restful and quiet.

Chapter Nineteen

Kim moved around slowly the next morning when she washed up and went down for breakfast. After carefully sitting at the table, Sadie brought her espresso and asked what she felt like eating.

"I'm not picky, Sadie. Whatever you have left over this morning is fine with me."

Nancy slipped in next to Kim and took a seat. "How is your pain now, Kim?"

Kim nibbled her bottom lip before replying that she felt no change in her pain level this morning and she was worried that the trial was a failure.

"Why don't you wait and see what Todd has to say at 10 am when he calls?" Nancy suggested. "This is the first day and you have the rest of the week to try different levels."

Kim could not argue that point with Nancy as she was right. She dug into her breakfast of scrambled eggs, bacon, flax, and whole grain toast.

Todd called right before 10 am. Kim felt like there was hope once again for the trial to work.

"Tell me your current pain level, Kim. Then we will go from there."

"Todd, I don't have any change in my pain level and that worries me." Kim fretted as she spoke.

"You are fine, Kim. Trust me. We are just getting started on this trial. Do you have your remote with you?"

"I have it in my hand. What do you want me to do?" Kim asked, hopeful that the trial would work.

"Push the power on button. That is the letter 'P', and you will see the lights and current settings on the remote."

"Now I want you to push the 'P' again and it will increase to the second small round light. Then push the 'up' arrow to change the lines at the top to level three. Do you have three lines showing, Kim?"

"Yes, Todd, I have the settings changed as you directed me to change them."

"Great! Now I want you to power the remote off. Tomorrow we will check how your pain level is and go from there. Changes will be made each day." Todd responded.

"Alright, thank you, and goodbye." Kim ended the call on her mobile phone. *Maybe I will feel less pain by tomorrow.* She prayed to Jesus silently, asking for His direction and what she should do.

Nancy asked Kim if she felt like driving into Evergreen to look around, but not to do anything that would cause problems with the trial or cause pain. Kim agreed.

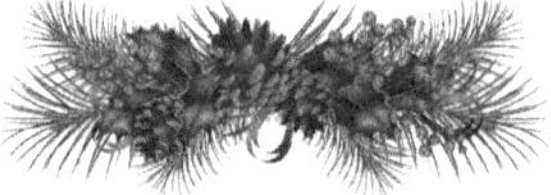

Nancy drove Kim's Jeep into Evergreen and they pulled up outside of Bain Lake Antiques. This store offered hard-to-find, unusual, and vintage antiques.

"They are big on unusual pieces," exclaimed Nancy as she gazed at an unusual timepiece. "The cabin and western décor are amazing. The shop is rather curious, indeed."

"Can we walk further inside, Nancy? I feel a need to walk just a bit." Kim gently stretched her back slightly.

"Of course, Kim. Today is at your pace." Nancy gave Kim a huge grin, then she yelled, "Check this out!" She had found the absolute perfect bed for her new house and master bedroom. The bed was created in solid dark oak with intricate carvings on the headboard.

Nancy paid for the bed, and the shop owners marked it as sold. When Nancy informed them of the move-in date of her new home, they were fine with the bed being picked up later.

Kim told Nancy that she needed a nap, so they left Evergreen for Lakewood.

Kim felt refreshed after her nap and then she realized that her pain level was down! Not by much, but it was different. Her legs tingled now and then, but 20 percent of her pain was gone! She went downstairs in a cautious manner, doing what her nurse and doctor had instructed.

She found both Leawood's and Nancy talking in the living room next to the children's playroom which was noisy and bubbling with the sounds of happy kids.

"How does your back feel?" Aaron inquired as all eyes turned to Kim, anxious, and wanting to hear something positive.

Sighing, Kim responded, "Well, I guess you must hear it at some point. Time to spill the beans, right? My pain is better! My legs tingle now and then, but my pain level is down by 20 percent!"

"That's wonderful," exclaimed Aaron. "Hopefully this will progress in the same direction. You need to reach 50 percent less pain for this trial to be considered good to go for a full surgical implant of wires and the device, under your skin on your lower back. You have several more days to reach that goal."

Nancy was thrilled to no end and Danny and Lisa came out to see what the fuss was about.

"Aunt Kim. Is your back better?"

"Yes, Danny," Kim smiled at both children, and she gave each one a huge hug.

Dinner and bedtime soon fell upon the household.

Chapter Twenty

Right on schedule, Kim's mobile rang at 10 am the next morning, Wednesday, day three of her trial device. It was Todd on the phone checking to see how Kim was doing and what her pain level was at.

"I honestly feel like my pain is 30 percent or so less this morning. I'm on track, right?"

"Yes, Kim, you are on track. Do you have the device remote?"

"Yes, I do. Should I turn it on now?" Kim asked.

"Yes. Do you see the settings we did yesterday?" Todd queried as he wrote the required notes for the trial. Daily notes had to be done for insurance purposes.

"This time I want you press the 'P' again and it will increase to the third small round light. Then push the 'up' arrow to change the lines at the top to level five. Can you tell me if you have it set?"

"I've got it set right and I can now power the remote off, correct?"

"Yes, again, Kim. I'll call you at 10 am tomorrow (Wednesday) morning. We will discuss how your back feels and change settings again. This is a trial-and-error process, but you're headed in the right direction."

After hanging up her call, Kim pondered what she could do today, and thought a little bit of walking would do her some good, if she was careful.

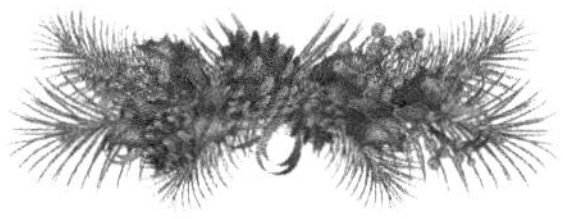

After lunch, Kim informed Sadie that she and Nancy planned to drive to the top of Lookout Mountain for the view. This would give the Leawood's family time at dinner.

Both women got out and walked on areas where the snow had been removed.

"I'll never, ever, tire of that gorgeous view to the west and the divide!" Nancy gushed and realized that relocating to Colorado was the best thing, ever, for them to do.

"The pines are lovely with the snow and the scent is heavenly. Look at the snowcapped peaks! Nancy, we did the right thing in moving here. I just feel it in my bones."

"Look at that sunset with the snowcapped mountains! Have we landed in heaven or what?" Nancy snapped photos of the setting sun.

"We best be head back down to Golden now, and we must watch for deer and elk on our winding way down Lookout Mountain." Kim sighed. "You are driving my Jeep, after all Nancy! "

On the way back down the mountain, they stopped at Woody Woods's Wood Fired Pizza, in Golden, for dinner, and shared a large Honey BBQ Chicken and Bacon pizza with extra Ham on top.

The meal was satisfying and the ride home in Kim's Jeep was an easy drive. They had no major traffic issues and when they arrived at the Leawood house, Aaron and Sarah were headed to bed. Both worked the next day, and the children were already asleep. Sadie and Alice had also gone home for the night.

"All okay today?" Sarah looked at Kim and Nancy.

"Today was perfect!" replied both women in unison.

Smiling that the day was perfect, everyone finally got to lay down and sleep.

Chapter Twenty-One

Kim's phone buzzed at 10 am. "Hi, Todd! So today is Thursday and day four of my device trial. Ask me how I am?"

"Good morning. You sound chipper. Tell me about your pain."

"I am chipper! I haven't felt this good in a very long time. My pain level has decreased by 45 percent. I feel great! Not great, but I feel much better!" Kim enthused as she smiled like a goofy nut case; delighted that her back pain was better than it had been for years.

"That's awesome, Kim. I'm so glad to hear this. Please grab your remote for your device and let's try a different setting today."

"I have my remote turned on now, Todd."

"Great! Do you see the settings we did yesterday?"

"Yes, Todd. What do you want me to do today?"

"Please press the 'P' until the fourth tiny round light is lit up. Change the up arow setting by pushing 'up' to change the lines at the top to level six. Do you have it set?"

"All good on my end, Todd."

"Today will be different, Kim. Today, I want you to start bending, and moving around more. I want you to gently, but purposefully, try to triggcr your back pain throughout the day."

"Why, Todd? No one told me that I was to challenge my pain during the trial. What is the purpose behind triggering my pain?"

"Your new settings will help you with your pain, Kim. We must see how you do with your pain triggered so we can truly tell if we are headed the right way." Todd explained.

"That makes sense. I powered the remote off."

"Perfect. I'll call you tomorrow, Friday at 10 am. Have a nice day," and Todd hung up.

Kim's phone rang again about 30 minutes later, and it was Erin, Dr. Paul's nurse. Erin asked how Kim was doing and that she was receiving daily reports from Todd along with his faxed written daily documentation; all which Dr. Paul viewed each morning.

"Dr. Smith thinks you will do well with the rest of the trial. We are both happy for you. I must go now; the office is busy." Erin reported before saying goodbye.

Kim was elated and informed Nancy of what Todd told her to do as far as to challenge and try to trigger her back pain. They were in the dining room alcove enjoying a late brunch of fresh fruit including Palisade peaches and grapes, and a chocolate croissant.

After finishing their meal, both helped clean up. Kim bent down to load the dishwasher, and she attempted to trigger her back pain, but it didn't work.

"Don't help me, Nancy. I need to repetitiously bend and unbend so I will do all the dishwasher loading and, I'll start it, too, as it is nearly full."

Nancy watched Kim do the morning chores carefully. She didn't want her friend to have pain or any kind of setback.

Chores done, Kim asked Nancy if she wanted to go shopping. Specifically, she wanted to know if Nancy was ready to at least look at, if not purchase, a new vehicle.

"Okay, Kim. I want to go to that huge dealership off I-70, Chrysler Jeep West. Since I've been driving your Jeep around during your trial, I've decided that I want to buy a Jeep this time."

Kim simply grinned at Nancy, as she could tell that her friend completely enjoyed her Jeep. Kim had made a "Jeep person" out of Nancy!

Nancy parked near the entrance to Chrysler Jeep West. After glancing around at the Jeeps in the showroom, Nancy asked for a brochure so she could see the options available.

The year 2024 Jeeps had been out already, and, after her catalog perusal, Nancy asked the salesman if she could build her own on their website. She wanted to build one with Kim and herself alone.

"You bet," replied the salesman. "Use this special tablet to see if anything strikes your fancy. All models and options are on the tablet. If you have questions, let me know."

After sitting comfortably on a sofa in the showroom, the women started looking at the tablet.

The first thing Nancy chose was a Jeep Grand Cherokee Limited like Kim's, yet newer, of course. "I love the Velvet Red Pearl-Coat Exterior Paint. Don't the 20" x 8.5" machined and painted aluminum wheels look nice?"

"I love your choice of color and the wheels. The wheels are more unusual than the ones I have on my Jeep. This is going to be fun deciding on what you want, Nancy!" Kim grinned at her best friend.

"It says the standard tire for that wheel is 265/60R18 BSW All-Season LRR Tires. They look huge; but I think I could get used to this pretty fast."

"Just wait, Nancy. You have many options to choose from including the interior." Kim knew Nancy was hooked on Jeeps. Both women laughed out loud, and the salesman gave them a smile.

"I like the Bright Side Steps better. Oh! Look at the Capri Leatherette Axis II Seats! I love the color combo and it comes with extra bells and whistles. That 10.1-inch touch screen Nav system is nice!" Nancy caught Kim's eye, "Your idea to shop for my new vehicle was superb, my friend."

"You have a few more options to choose from, Nancy. But know that heated seats are awesome, especially in Colorado!" Kim laughed.

"Oh, Kim! I've not had this much fun in a long time. To do this with my best friend and soul sister means the world to me." Nancy gave Kim a hug.

Amplified speakers, subwoofer, and the dual-pane panoramic sunroof were option upgrades, and Nancy chose both for her new Jeep.

Nancy went with the standard engine, transmission, and suspension for this model.

By the time Nancy was finished with her choices, she had more electricals and options in the Jeep than she ever had with other vehicles she'd owned.

Nancy particularly liked the Integrated Off-Road Camera, Power Tilt / Telescope Steering Column, Rain-Sensitive Windshield Wipers, Rear Back-Up Camera Washer, Surround View Camera System, and Ventilated Front Seats. Comfort and safety were top priorities, and the rest was icing on the cake.

A price was settled on, and Nancy paid for her new Jeep in full. Her custom Jeep would take two months to deliver.

"You handed that salesman a huge Christmas bonus, Nancy, and he didn't even have to try to sell you anything!" Both giggled.

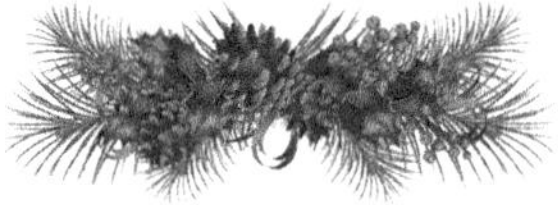

Back at the Leawood home, Alice was helping Sadie finish a salad to go with dinner. All of them would be at the dinner table tonight.

After everyone gathered at the dinner table, grace was said, and they shared a meal of side salad, and a nice, thick, and chunky beef stew with homemade rolls. Pure comfort food. Pure comfort to the end of another perfect winter day in Colorado with family and friends.

Chapter Twenty-Two

Right on schedule, Todd called at 10 am Friday morning. Kim antic-ipated his call and had her mobile in her left hand and her device remote in her right hand. Excitement permeated and bubbled through and around Kim, catching the entire household in her happiness.

"Good morning, Kim. How do you feel today?" Todd asked.

Nancy, Alice, and Sadie watched expectantly for Kim's answer as she had been mysterious about her pain level this morning.

"My pain level is down a good 60 percent! This device works! I'm so happy and thrilled to find something to help my pain at long last." Kim excitedly informed Todd.

Nancy, Alice, and Sadie sported huge grins on their faces.

"Wow, Kim! That's great news! The goal of the trial was to decrease your pain level by 50 percent or greater and you surpassed that! I will document everything and let Dr. Smith know. You can leave the settings as they are, Kim."

"Thank you, Todd! I have a new lease on life!"

"I'm thrilled that you had success with the trial. Dr. Smith will be in touch. Goodbye and Merry Christmas!"

"Merry Christmas, Todd." Kim hung up the call.

It was December after all, and soon she would move into her home and gallery in Evergreen.

Not 30 minutes had passed when Kim received a call from Dr. Paul's nurse, Erin.

"Good morning, Erin."

"Good morning, Kim. Dr. Smith is thrilled that the nerve stimulator device has proved to be effective in helping the pain in your back."

"As the one who has suffered relentlessly, I bet I'm happier than he is."

"This is day five of the trial. Some trials are five days and others are six days. We planned on six days, but Dr. Smith wondered if you wanted the trial device removed this afternoon around 1 pm. Does that agree with you, Kim?"

"It sure does! I'll be there right before 1 pm. See you later!" Kim hung up the call.

Then Kim asked Sadie not to prepare dinner tonight as Kim wanted to make dinner for her hosts. She'd missed cooking since leaving Boston. This time, Nancy would be her co-conspirator in the kitchen.

Nancy pulled the Jeep up to Dr. Paul Smith's clinic five minutes early. This morning had been monumental, to say the least. Kim checked in and the wait began.

Erin called Kim's name a few minutes after 1 pm, and she followed her into an examination room.

"I need to obtain your vital signs and document your pain level. How is your pain doing now?" Erin placed a blood pressure cuff and pulse oximeter on Kim.

"I'm down 60 percent and I feel like I now have a new lease on life."

"Wonderful. Dr. Smith will be in shortly to see you." Erin closed the exam room door as she left the room.

Dr. Paul…as the Leawood children called him, came in a few minutes later… I'm supposed to call him Paul as he'd requested…Kim wanted to melt into his arms…get a grip, Kim…romance now? Just over one month since the tragedies in Boston? Unbelievable! Yet, here Kim was, and she drowned in the depths of Paul's dark blue eyes…how could I be drawn to a man so soon? This attraction I've never felt before…Unbelievable!

Paul felt doomed, in a good way, as he stared into Kim's green eyes...she is my downfall, is she 'the one'...Kim simply is...stay professional, Paul...Kim was fast going from friend to romance if he had anything to say about it...stay professional for this doctor's visit...the future will come about if it is meant to be...

The moment broke as Paul cleared his throat. "Tell me about your pain level, Kim, and what you did to trigger your pain to start."

"I'm down 60 percent of my pain, I moved around and walked, and I bent over repetitiously to place items in the dishwasher, which is something that I had to give up due to pain in the past. Did I do enough triggers?" Kim desperately wanted to know his answer.

"Yes, you did fine, Kim." Dr. Smith replied as he documented in her computer medical record.

"I'll remove each layer of dressing and bandages, then I will slip the wires out of your back. The removal is not too painful."

He gently removed the dressings and then slowly withdrew the wires.

"You have a single drop of spinal fluid at the insertion site. I will cover it with a small dressing, and you can take it off and enjoy a shower later this evening, but no bath or jacuzzi until tomorrow. How does that sound?" Dr. Smith smiled at Kim.

Dang, I have it bad. This woman amazes me every time I see her. And I want to see her again, soon.

"Sounds great, Dr. Paul. By the way, I'm cooking dinner at the Leawood home this evening. Would you like to join us? The meal is set for 7 pm, but you can come ahead of time, if you don't have plans already since it is a Friday, after all." Kim held her breath as she waited for an answer.

"You cook, too? I won't pass that up. You can count me in!" Paul smiled at Kim. "You are all done here, now."

"Thank you," Kim replied as she left the exam room, grabbed her Jeep keys from Nancy in the lobby, and left the clinic. They headed to the grocery store for the special items Kim needed for dinner.

Chapter Twenty-Three

*C*hef Kim took over the kitchen with Nancy as her sous chef. Kim had planned a simple meal, not elegant, but comfort food instead. The Leawood's had been serving comfort food since the women arrived, and it felt great to be back in the kitchen cooking.

Kim had been itching for a taste of chicken-fried steak, made her way, with homemade mashed potatoes with real gravy made from pan drippings, French green beans, side vegetable sticks with homemade hummus dip, homemade rolls, and lemon pudding pie with blueberries for dessert.

The rolls were baking as Kim pounded a tenderized cut of beef into a half and half mixture of flour and corn flake crumbs with a bit of salt and pepper. Then she dipped it into a mixture of eggs and milk, followed by smacking down in the dry mixture once more. Kim preferred pan frying over deep frying as she could use the pan drippings for true homemade gravy.

As sous chef, Nancy was tasked with the homemade mashed potatoes, French green beans, and slicing the fresh vegetables for dipping in the hummus she had made.

"Nancy, my back sure is hurting. Can you grab an icy hot patch for me, please?"

"As sous chef, and your substitute nurse, I hereby declare one patch coming right up." Nancy grabbed a patch and placed it on her friend.

"It's a good thing I'm your sous chef," Nancy added. "You can't do this meal alone. I will set the table and when the meal is done, you must sit down, and I will have Sadie help me carry the platters to the table."

Kim nodded in the affirmative.

Kim kept the graham cracker crust, lemon pudding pie, and fresh blueberries cold in the fridge.

With the meal half done, Kim heard the bell for the front door and Aaron opened it and welcomed Paul inside.

"Something cooking sure smells good." Paul commented as he took his outerwear off before sitting down near the fireplace. Everyone was gathered in the living room, and a 9-foot-tall artificial balsam spruce Christmas tree sat in the corner.

The meal was just about ready when Nancy went out to ask Sadie for a bit of help in serving the platters laden with food.

Nancy and Sadie brought platters of food to the table, while the others claimed their seats, and a large gravy boat full of rich homemade gravy. This way each person could use how much gravy they wanted for their steak and potatoes.

Balsam scented candles with fake greenery burned as a centerpiece on the table, and the look was festive.

Once Nancy and Sadie took their seats, Aaron said grace and the meal began.

Paul sat next to Kim. Smiling, he asked, "How does your back feel?"

"Not good. The pain is quite high. I think I need the implanted nerve stimulator surgery. Is that a surgery you can do, Paul?" Kim grimaced in pain, and everyone noticed her expression and response to Paul.

"Dr. Paul, I thought you had fixed Aunt Kim's back. Why does Aunt Kim's back hurt? Did you not fix her back right?" Danny demanded an answer from him.

"Lower your voice, Danny, and ask questions in a nice way, please." Aaron gave Danny a stern look.

"Let me try to explain, Danny. I placed a test device in Kim for her back pain. It was a test only and it had to come out today. Now that we know it works, a new one can be placed in surgery." Paul glanced over to Aaron then back to Danny.

"So, Aunt Kim needs surgery?" Danny's eyes widened. "Will it hurt? Will you do the surgery?"

"I want to know, too. Aunt Kim's back has hurt her too long!" Lisa stared at Uncle Paul with a questioning look on her face.

"How about we eat dinner first and this discussion can be resumed after dinner, okay?" Aaron spoke as he looked at the two children.

"Kim will be okay soon, I promise." Paul told both Danny and Lisa.

The meal commenced and Kim and Paul smiled a small secret smile at each other, which perked up Nancy's attention.

Sarah informed Kim that she had to give her the secret to making crispy and tender, yet fork and regular knife cutting, chicken-fried steaks. The lemon pudding pie with fresh blueberries was a hit with everyone and Kim wasn't allowed to help with the cleanup or loading the dishwasher.

Instead, Kim and Paul sat together in the breakfast nook alone. Paul placed one hand over Kim's which gave her tingles, of a good kind.

Kiss me Paul...do it now...I want a sweet and tender kiss...not the slobbery kind...sweet and delicious...a forever kiss...a soft kiss...a tender kiss that makes me melt...

"Kim, you can have a permanent nerve stimulator placed, if you desire. It would be at least a week before it can fit into the surgery schedule. Surgery is rather booked up this time of year with ski accidents, and people falling on ice keep the operating rooms hopping."

"I do, Paul." Kim looked into Paul's eyes and melted. "I trust you to do the right work on my back and I know you will." Kim sighed as she leaned toward his shoulder, without a care as to who saw them in such a cozy position.

Kim was done hiding her feelings for Paul...she knew now that love can happen faster than fast...swift...my face must show how hard I've fallen for Paul...yet...

she could not let this amazing, gentle, and kind man get away from her...lost in his soul-searching eyes…

"I want you to know that I've fallen in love with you, and I think you have similar feelings. Right? I know it's crazy for it to happen this fast, but for me it has done that. You are the man I've been needing, but didn't know I needed, until…now." Then Kim kissed Paul's cheek before giving him a hug.

I belong in this man's arms...forever and ever…and ever, again...into eternity!

Gently cupping Kim's face, Paul gave her the sweetest kiss that proved he loved her, too. "You've knocked me over with your beauty, inside and out, your sense of humor, your courage and fortitude, and you being you, not fake, and not looking for a meal ticket."

Paul kept Kim embraced in his arms, giving himself to her, in his own way, to make her feel the love of his heart beating madly for her, and her alone.

"I know many things must be done in the next few weeks, but I'm here for you, always, Kim." Paul murmured into Kim's ear.

Before they parted, they shared a deeper kiss so Kim could go rest her back and Paul left for home.

Romance...knock my socks off…or all my clothes…Kim thought…yes, good idea…get a grip, Kim…you are NOT a lovesick teenager…yet Paul will be mine… I know it...I know it in my soul…no one has ever affected me this way…Paul will be mine…I never felt this way with Steve…that was a different love…or lust…not true love…but this, with Paul, is a true love down to my very core…I finally know what true love feels like…and it can happen at first sight…

Headed for home, Paul knew it was just a matter of time before Kim was his… yes, she would be, and soon…humming to the Christmas music flowing through the speakers of his Land Rover…but her back needed work…the pain must subside... Kim's grimaces of pain when she thought no one was looking tore at his insides… priorities are first…then Kim would be his…true love at long last…and Kim was worth the wait...Kim was spectacular! I'm going to make her mine!

Chapter Twenty-Four

On Saturday morning, Kim and Nancy prepared for move-in day in Kim's condo and her art gallery. It was closing day! December 10 had snuck up fast. Kim had gratefully accepted help from Nancy, of course, the Leawood's, and Paul. Even Alice and Sadie got in on the act!

Kim's Jeep was loaded full as was Paul's Range Rover and, of course, the Leawood's brought their vehicle loaded with the children, Alice, and Sadie.

Nancy asked Kim if she needed a patch placed and Kim nodded yes. "Yes, Nurse Nancy, please." Kim sighed. While Nancy got the patch Kim and Paul exchanged glances. It was time to decide on the direction Kim wanted to go regarding surgery and placement of a permanent nerve stimulator.

"I do, Paul. I want the surgery as soon as possible. My pain is quite bad, more and more lately. It's not quality of life. I'm so tired of pain every single day. It never, ever stops!"

"You decided to do it? Oh, Kim, I've been praying you would get the permanent nerve stimulator." Nancy placed the new icy hot patch on Kim's lower back.

Paul handed a package to Kim. She withdrew a black belt of sorts. Then he showed Kim how to use it around her lumbar back to help give more support.

The special belt had boning sewn into the back of it for additional support. The belt came together in the front and was held in place with VELCRO®. On each side double wide strong elastic bands cinched the belt tighter and used VELCRO®.

"Try using it for three hours or less until you get a better idea of how it best suits you. Shall we bundle up and head for Evergreen everyone?"

"Beat you out the door, Uncle Paul." Danny ran to the door, and he arrived first, followed by Paul and Lisa. Laughter had thus commenced. Today would be a good day.

Nancy drove Kim's Jeep up to Evergreen so that Kim could ride up the canyon with Paul. As Paul and his dreamy eyes drove, Kim admired him slyly, or so she thought. Paul gave Kim a wink and with that – so much for slyly checking him out.

Man, oh man, I want this man badly...not just for sex, either...I bet he's hot in bed...a perfect lover...yet what I most love is his kind and caring soul...and he doesn't lie to me...or hide anything from me...I wonder if marriage is a possibility? Slow down, Kim! Why rush a great thing? But I must rush... I don't want to lose him...but I don't want to scare him away, either...

"You know what, Kim?" Paul asked as he drove up the curvy mountain canyon.

"I have no idea of your thoughts. What's up?" Kim wanted to know as she eyed Paul with suspicion. "Do you have something planned? Something I'm the last to find out about?" She looked at Paul with a sly smile, before breaking into giggles. Teasing Paul was fun.

"Aaron and I both have Sunday, December 11, off. If I can get an anesthesiologist to come in, you could have surgery tomorrow, on your back, in and out the same day, and Aaron and I could attend the surgery together. If you want to, that is..."

"Yes!" Kim interrupted Paul and replied in less than a nanosecond, her eyes gleaming with hope. "Thank you, Lord Jesus, for this most splendid chance to reduce my pain."

"Well, okay, then," Paul laughed. On call surgical nurses were on standby so that would work out nicely. Paul and Aaron had already decided to not charge Kim for their services, so it would be less for Kim to pay. As it was, out of pocket for Kim would be a minimum of $30 thousand since she had no insurance.

Dear Lord, I want Kim's pain to be better handled, better managed…and I want Kim…with me…beside me…in my home…in my bed…when her back is better…I'm totally smitten, and the love bug has struck…I want to marry Kim soon! I have the perfect ring for her…a lovely designer ring that had been my mother's…a 4.28 Carat Pear Shaped Diamond with French Cut Pavé Diamonds down both shanks…in yellow gold…Kim would be his wife if he had any say in the matter!

Chapter Twenty-Five

*U*pon reaching Kim's condo, Paul unlocked the door. When the men brought in boxes for Kim and Nancy, the movers arrived with their belongings from Boston. Perfect timing. Kim had her new home, and her new gallery. Life was looking pretty darn good!

The movers didn't have much to bring in as the women had packed personal items, clothing, and accessories, linens, and they had sold their furniture when they sold their respective homes in Boston. Nancy directed the movers in the placement of the boxes.

"Please wait a few minutes before heading to the gallery." Kim asked the movers if they would like some coffee and they said yes. Coffee would be a nice warm up and break.

Sadie made coffee in the kitchen while Kim showed the condo to the rest, especially her and Nancy's bedrooms, as that was where Alice and Sadie would place their clothing, bathroom supplies, makeup, bed linens, and the like, to prepare for the women's first night in Evergreen – tonight!

How I wish I was staying here in that bed with Kim tonight…I'd take things gently and make it easy on her back…I love Kim and the closeness we share…the friendship we share…that exploded into true love…her scoliosis doesn't bother me in the least…some people look at it as a disability…some people look down on those who aren't perfect…I only see Kim…the woman I love…

I wish Paul was able to stay tonight….Nancy will be here, but Paul could hold me close all night long…we could talk…I've fallen hard for him…hook, line, and sinker…Paul is kind, honest, caring, has dreamy eyes, and a great body…Paul accepts me as I am with my scoliosis and bad back…he loves me that much…Paul accepts my flaws…he never judges me…I love him so much that it hurts to not be near him…

Sarah commented that the personal elevator should help Kim out a lot and everyone loved the condo.

Then Sarah responded that she had a date with Danny and Lisa skating on the lake and they left to skate. The children were excited as it was their first time to skate this year. Sarah was excited to see the enjoyment on their faces.

Sarah loved the little blended family that she and Aaron had created. She missed her boys in heaven, but she also knew she was blessed with the family she had upon the beautiful blue sphere of life named Earth.

"Later, Aaron." Sarah kissed him goodbye and the three took off for the lake.

The movers followed the Land Rover and Jeep to the art gallery. Once there, Kim unlocked the front door and invited everyone inside. The movers brought in their cargo and left.

"Wow, Kim! This is a nice gallery, and it overlooks the lake here in the Heart of Evergreen." Paul commented as he hugged Kim and gave her a soft kiss. "Congratulations!"

"Thank you, everyone! My dream has come to fruition." Kim smiled as she glanced around the gallery.

"Shall we start unwrapping art pieces, Nancy, so the guys can hang them where we think they will show off best? You know how we discussed this and how I had my gallery in Boston."

"I'm on it, Kim! Why don't you unwrap the sculptures and place them where you want them in the locked glass display cases while we handle the larger art and their placement?"

"Yes, Nurse Nancy," Kim agreed.

With that, they all got busy setting up the gallery while Kim arranged the glass cases and managed to remember how to work the cash register. Kim made coffee and had brough cookies for a snack, and everyone dug right in when they took a break.

"I love the art you created, Kim. You are one heck of a creative lady! I am awestruck. Your pieces blend in well with the other pieces on display from your commission pieces. You have impressed me once again. It there anything you can't do?" Paul commented and then laughed. Everyone joined in the laughter.

"Well, I've not decided on a name for the gallery, but Nancy and I plan to open it with a huge gallery showing for not only my pieces, but for all the art housed and sold here from local artisans."

Ideas on names were tossed around until Kim had a gleam in her eye and her new gallery name. "How about 'The Gallery Loft of Evergreen'? I have a loft with more pieces on display. See this wood carving here? The wood carver is Richard Manse, a local in Evergreen. I'll commission a sign for the gallery from him!" Kim smiled in satisfaction, happy with the new name and her new gallery.

"Perfect!" Nancy exclaimed, and then she showed the loft to both men while Kim rested her back. When they came back down, Nancy saw Kim grimace and went into 'Nurse Nancy' mode and placed a new icy hot patch on Kim's lower back.

Satisfied with how her gallery looked, she locked up and they all went back to Kim's condo.

Wafting from the kitchen was a scent of chili that drew the four of them into the kitchen where Sadie and Alice were busy making nourishment. Sarah and both kids watched the snow start to fall again and an elk came into view.

"Check that elk out!" Danny was excited and it was contagious.

They settled down to dinner of chili with cheese and fresh tomato slices. Nancy did the clean-up and the Leawood's said goodbye and headed for Lakewood and home with two sleepy children. Paul was not far behind them in his Land Rover.

Nestled in bed, both women fell asleep, happy to spend their first night in Evergreen. *Tomorrow will take care of itself...*

Chapter Twenty-Six

With Nancy riding shotgun, Kim drove her Jeep down the canyon the next morning. She parked at the clinic in Lakewood and met up with Aaron and Paul.

Paul's nurse, Erin, welcomed the women and led them to a pre-op room.

Kim undressed and put on a hospital gown and slide proof socks on her feet, before diving underneath the covers on the gurney bed. Kim didn't dive exactly (her back prevented that) as she bent to get under the bedding for warmth. Pre-Op, OR, and Post-Op were notoriously kept cold so that germs and bacteria growth was inhibited.

Erin took Kim's vital signs and inserted a 20 gauge IV into her right hand. Kim was placed on telemetry and normal saline fluids dripped in slow, she was given her initial Versed, after she signed the paperwork for the surgery.

The anesthesiologist, Dr. Timmons, came in and looked inside Kim's mouth for loose teeth (they all do this) and throat (to see if they have clear access in case of need for intubation), and he asked Kim if she had any loose teeth or partial plates. Then he informed Kim of the anesthesia that would be used and checked her medicine allergies.

When the scrub tech arrived, Kim was wheeled to the OR and Nancy was escorted to the lobby to wait until the surgery was completed.

Kim slid over to the OR table and turned onto her stomach. The anesthesiologist then gave her the anesthesia.

The next thing Kim knew, she woke up in the post-op area and the internal sterile electrodes and device had been placed, the surgery was over and done with.

Dr. Paul read what was done to Kim and Nancy. "The device is in correct placement, and the electrical pulses higher in your back mask the pain signal in your lower back. You have a small incision in your lower back and another near your right side at waist level. This is where the device/generator was placed under your skin. Any questions?"

"I'm good," Kim replied, and Nancy nodded in agreement and smiled at her friend. Then she looked at Paul with sheer admiration on her face. Kim knew her back pain was reduced, finally.

"The stimulator is controlled with a small hand-held remote, just like the one you used in your trial. The settings are adjustable, and they are currently set on the level that we start each patient on. You won't feel any real relief just yet." Paul gave Kim a tender look as he saw she was still rather sleepy.

"Do you have any questions, Nancy? I don't think Kim will remember everything discussed."

"I'm good so far," replied Nancy as she smiled at Kim. "Plus, you are giving us the handouts that explain what you are telling us, right?"

"Correct. We double and triple teach patients to make sure all is understood. Okay, then, Kim's generator is a rechargeable type and the batteries average 10 – 15 years or a bit more. Sterile electrodes were placed and then anchored by sutures to minimize movement." Paul smiled down at Kim.

"I need to see you move your feet, Kim." Kim complied. "Next, Erin will assist you in a short walk and to use the bathroom."

Kim passed the walking test and she voided, before she walked back to the gurney, and she sat in a chair next to the gurney bed. On her table was ice water and graham crackers, so she ate and drank without sickness to her stomach. Third and final hurdle passed!

"You look awesome, Kim! I know, for a fact, that you now have a new lease on life, and I'm so happy for you," Nancy said with tears in her eyes. "My friend turned sister will finally have some pain management relief."

Erin went over discharge instructions and Nancy signed the paperwork. She then removed the IV and let Kim remove the telemetry pads herself as she remembered Kim was sensitive to adhesive.

Once redressed in the clothes she'd worn into the clinic, a wheelchair was brought in, Kim was wheeled out to her Jeep, and assisted inside the front passenger seat. Nancy drove Kim back to Evergreen in softly falling snow.

I wish I was able to go with them…Kim leaving for home, and I must care for my patients…she will never be free from back pain…her back is too messed up for that…but that pain can be managed and reduced…I love that gorgeous woman… until we see each other again…I miss that wonderful coconut scent of her hair…I want to run my fingers through her hair…

Nancy cooked a light dinner for the two of them, chicken noodle soup and grilled cheese sandwiches. She monitored Kim closely, which was mostly Kim dozing off. Kim slept not so much from the surgery, but because she knew her back pain would be better, for the rest of her days on planet Earth. She was content at last, not free from pain, but she knew her pain would be manageable, yet she hurt and wished Paul was with her and Nancy.

I miss Paul so much…I know Jesus brought Paul into my life for more than medical purposes…He knew we would fall in love…soulmates…and he helps many patients…a truly caring doctor…a great neurosurgeon…my man…the tingles from his sweet kisses…the electricity we have together…Paul is amazing…

Kim was grateful; she thanked Jesus for what He did for her and continued to do for her. Her pain management would work, she knew it, and she was thankful.

Paul called that evening to check on Kim, and they spoke for a while on the phone, mostly talking about each other and getting to know one another better until Kim fell asleep with her phone in her hand. Paul smiled and hung up his phone when he heard Kim snore softly.

The next morning, Nancy drove Kim's Jeep once again to the clinic in Lakewood. Dr. Paul saw Kim for a post-op visit and she was directed to set her settings on the remote for her device. The final trial settings were used, the ones that had worked best for Kim.

Under advisement, and doctor orders, Kim rested and took things easy that week. She missed Paul something fierce and wondered when she would see him again. He was a busy neurosurgeon, after all, and patients had to be taken care of. They still had evenings when they spoke on the phone, laughing, loving, and learning about each other. It was divine!

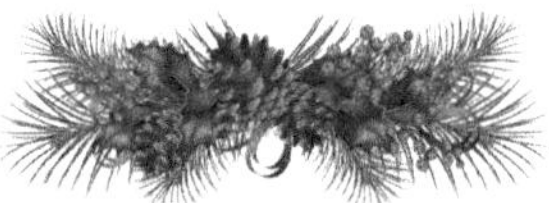

On Tuesday, Nancy went to the gallery to check things out and she made a phone call to Richard Manse, an Evergreen local, known for his amazing wood carvings.

Richard Manse knocked on the gallery front door, and Nancy opened the door. "Hi. I'm Richard Manse, and I've come to see about creating a sign for your gallery."

"Good morning. I'm Nancy. Please come in and take a seat over there," she pointed to the coffee table area before pouring a cup of coffee for each of them. "I'll be right back with what is needed for the business logo signage."

Richard stared at Nancy's butt as she went to the back room for the drawings.

Nancy was a perfect petite woman with curves galore and short dark pixie cut hair... this is certainly a rather interesting day...she looks to be in her mid-20s and I'm 31...not much of an age difference...but why am I drawn to her? She's cute! That's why! I must ask her for a date, after I make the signage for the business...I can't get her heart shaped butt out of my head...aching for my touch...or maybe I ache to touch her...

Nancy laid the drawings on the counter near the coffee pot and told Richard. "The new name of the gallery is 'The Gallery Loft of Evergreen'. How does that sound to you?"

Richard was tall, over six feet, dark hair with a neatly trimmed beard, like a mountain man should be...his eyes a startling shade of blue...handsome for sure! Just like a mountain man should be...talk about a great physique – not one ounce of fat on him...gosh...Kim had found Paul...Have I found my new man, too? I hope so....he might be about age 30 or so...perfect....so dang handsome...no other man could ever look as good as Richard!

"Great name for your gallery. I want to thank you for continued support in hosting my art works sold on commission." He smiled at Nancy, and she smiled back.

"You are most welcome. By the way, I'm not the gallery owner but her assistant-in-chief. I handle anything and everything that comes our way, but I'm not an artist. Care for another cup of coffee?" Nancy queried Mr. Tall, Dark, and Handsome.

"Sure, nothing better on a cold morning." Richard smiled down at Nancy. A kiss would warm me up fast, he thought.

"I have an idea on the type of wood to use for the outdoor gallery signage. Red cedar wood works well in the elements outdoors, especially if weatherproofed after staining. I think a water-based clear polyurethane would do the job. How does that sound?"

"Sounds perfect. Kim wants the signage to be carved like the sign the previous owners used. Can that be done?" Nancy peered up at Richard's gorgeous face and smiled. Those amazing eyes!

"You bet! I made that sign for them. The carving and painting of the lettering takes time but looks nice after a stain and waterproofing. Polyurethane is easy to apply and leaves a nice protective and clear finish." Richard stole a quick look at Nancy while her head was turned down, reading the specs for the sign.

"How long do you think it will take? We plan to host a grand opening/open house/art show on the Friday before Christmas. That's December 23." I wonder if his beard is scratchy when kissed? Yes, this mountain man works for me. Guess I'm a mountain kind of girl!

"I'll have it done and hung by December 20. Any other specs I need to know?" Richard boldly winked at Nancy, and she blushed. A cute little blush and he caused it.

"Sounds great. By the way, I love those carved nativity and cardinals you created. The ones in the center glass case." Nancy pointed to the case.

"Thank you. Those are my favorite pieces to carve since I'm of the Christian faith."

"I knew you were a Christian man when I saw those pieces. I'm also Christian." Nancy added as an afterthought.

"I had best be going if that sign gets hung by December 20. Catch you then, right?" Richard gave Nancy another wink and she smiled openly, no blush this time.

Nancy locked up the gallery and drove back to Kim's condo with a peaceful smile on her face and she wondered how long she could hide her thoughts about Richard from Kim.

Chapter Twenty-Seven

The days flew by fast as the final gallery displays, special lighting, and security cameras were installed. Everyone was busy doing one thing or another at work and when home.

Nancy had sent out fancy invitations to those artists showcased in the gallery and all-around Evergreen, Lakewood, and beyond. She had created the design using the signage of 'The Gallery Loft of Evergreen' and, despite her denials, her own artistic abilities had shown brightly to all.

Kim and Paul chatted on the phone every evening, and the best part was that the nerve stimulation device had lowered Kim's lumbar back pain by 65 percent! Kim had a new lease on life, and she was also blessed with Paul in her life. He deeply thanked the Lord for Kim's pain level decrease, and they on their mobiles every evening and into the early morning hours about their love, life, hopes, and dreams.

Kim and Paul had secret plans immediately after the gallery showing ended, special plans that included the loved ones in their lives; those who'd be attending the gallery showing. Plans set in motion when Nancy wasn't home, so she didn't know that Kim had snuck off with Paul for three necessary items needed when they locked the gallery doors. They both struggled to keep their mission secret.

Nancy was busy with the gallery and getting the new signage up and secured in place in front of the gallery. Richard and Nancy had more time to chat, and she gave him her phone number, but had not gone out on a date yet. That issue would soon change, and they both knew it. Richard even secured the Christmas lights on the outside of the gallery and all outside décor – he was a creative person after all.

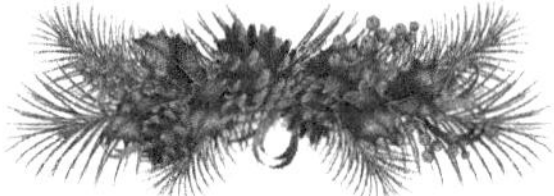

December 23 arrived on schedule! The plan was to open the gallery at 3 pm for the grand opening, open house, and art show. It was all hands-on deck! Kim knew that countless numbers of visitors and artists would be present. She was ready. The three-hour show was set to close at 6 pm.

The women were decked out in formal winter dresses of heavy fabrics such as suede, tweed, and velvet creations mixed with faux fur wraps or shrugs (when outdoors), and heels.

Kim's dress of emerald, green velvet trimmed in faux fur around the neckline matched her green eyes; as did her emerald, green winter boots. Kim chose diamond and pearl drop earrings as her only accessory. Earrings that she'd bought for herself, regal, yet understated. Her green eyes shimmered in the gallery lighting.

"I want to slide that gown off you right now," Paul whispered in Kim's ear. Paul was dapper in his own dark blue blazer with a matching scarf around his neck for warmth. Black leather boots completed his look, and a gold watch surrounded his left wrist.

"And I want to sink into your fathomless dark eyes and never resurface," added Kim. She smiled at the guests and other artists. "Do you think anyone is suspicious of our secret? Have they picked up on anything?"

"Nope! Not even a little bit! I'm going to love every single inch of your body tonight!" Paul gave her a grin, and she smiled back.

"Promises, promises, but never any action." Kim grinned back in a teasing manner. Truly, they had yet to make love but planned to eliminate that fact quite soon. After a brief kiss, both went to mingle with their guests and the other artists.

Nancy wore a sleek, red silk dress that flared out from the knees down. The heart-shaped neckline fit snug and secure yet showed off every curve of her body. The sleeves flowed down to her wrists. Red heels and a diamond pendant with matching earrings finished her stunning look.

Richard wore a mountain man look; a suit made of denim, and a rugged sheepskin vest for warmth. His brown leather boots shone in the gallery lighting and his beard was meticulously trimmed. Rugged handsomeness defined him in five syllables.

"That dress hugs each of your curves, woman! I don't think it's legal." Richard gave Nancy a wink and a small slap on her rear before heading off to guests looking at his carvings. I wonder if she liked that little slap on her butt. That heart-shaped butt is my downfall, and I don't even care.

Richard is the best thing to ever happen in my life…and I'm giddy in love…I know it must be true love as our feelings are deeper than simple lust…plus, we've never had sex yet…My butt still tingles…in a good way…not pain…but tingles of warmth and electricity flowed throughout her body and blood…

Aaron Leawood dressed in a tasteful yet casual dark blue suit with tie, and Sarah wore a floor length dress in dark blue velvet and matching pumps. Danny and Lisa sported Christmas colors of red and green. Attending a gallery showing was a first for all four of them.

Aaron's mom wore a teal floor length dress made of chiffon with matching flats, and Sadie decided on a raspberry floor length linen gown and matching flats. Both wore pearl necklaces and earrings. They had special duties later in the evening, and they managed not to spill the beans.

Everyone knew their job for the event, and they were ready, whether they poured champagne, hot apple cider, hot cocoa, fresh coffee, or mint tea.

Small serving plates were next to each charcuterie board with napkins and mini forks, knives, and skewers. Each charcuterie board scattered about the gallery contained food fit for a king. Each board was different in their set up, but the main components included displays of all kinds of meats, hard cheeses, dried and fresh fruits, and vegetables, toasted nuts, plus complementary condiments like honeys, jams, jellies, chutneys, mustards and more!

The door was unlocked and the traditional art as well as the Avant Garde pieces shone brightly. Artists that were present greeted those who ventured inside the gallery.

The showing was a huge success. More than 75 percent of the gallery pieces had sold and been taken to their new homes by 5:30 pm. Clean-up went fast and soon the gallery was spic and span, and in need of new art designs to grace the walls, gleam behind glass cases, and Kim knew that it would soon fill up again with the feedback she'd received throughout the event.

Chapter Twenty-Eight

It was showtime! Paul locked the gallery door and Nancy looked at him with confusion written on her face.

"This showing was successful. How about a glass of champagne or cider? After all, it's only us in here now." Paul queried with a huge smile. In the corner, another man stood, still and quiet, and not part of their social circle.

Nancy pointed discreetly to the other man and Paul brushed her off and dismissed her concern. That puzzled her further and she headed over to Kim to find out what the heck was going on.

"It's okay, Nancy," Kim smiled at her friend. "No worries about the other man. He's harmless. Truly"

"Okay, what is going on? Spill the secret beans now." Nancy whispered in Kim's ear.

"Nope! Can't do that! You must wait and watch." Kim walked over to Paul, and he cleared his throat.

"Kim and I have three special announcements. Please hold off all toasts until you hear and see our news."

With that Paul got down on one knee, looked up at Kim with complete adoration on his face, and asked, "Will you marry me, Kim?" He held out an antique sparkling marquise-cut diamond engagement ring that had once belonged to his mother.

"Yes, Paul. I will marry you." She laughed as he slipped the sparkling ring on her ring finger, it fit perfectly, and they kissed.

The special announcement number one was now completed. Everyone congratulated them and offered toasts. Until…

"Hello." The gentleman who'd been in the corner cleared his throat, and everyone looked at him, as he stood next to Kim and Paul.

"We are gathered here in the company of family and friends to marry Kim Daily and Dr. Paul Smith…I now pronounce you man and wife. You may kiss the bride." The special announcement number two was now completed.

Now that was a show! The Evergreen preacher had married them, and everyone was glowing with happiness. The toasting for the happy couple was delivered, and the children squealed with delight. Aaron and Nancy signed as witnesses. Everyone beamed with pure love and happiness.

"I'm thrilled to the max! But, how in the world did you get this done so fast? And how in the world did you pull this off without me knowing something was up with you two?" Nancy asked as she sipped her champagne.

"A Colorado marriage license does not have a waiting period, so we grabbed the license in Evergreen secretly yesterday and now we are married!" Paul answered, with his arm around Kim's waist in a possessive nature.

My bride! Paul was delirious with happiness and knew his life was now complete, as did Kim.

Paul elaborated further and explained that a Colorado marriage license does not have a waiting period, which means you can get the license, and get married in the same day.

Although Catholic, Kim and Paul had decided to marry this way, with all family and friends present, and they planned to have their marriage blessed in the Catholic Church they attended in Lakewood. This way, they didn't need to go through the six months of teaching and marriage counseling that was required to marry in the Catholic church.

Kim asked everyone to bundle up warm as it was time to leave the gallery and head out to the waiting sleighs.

Wait! What? The children squealed with delight when they spotted the waiting sleighs, with Christmas lights aglow and bells tinkling from around the horses' necks, through the windows.

No one had seen them pull up during the ceremony as all eyes were engrossed on Kim and Paul, and the magical wedding ceremony. The special announcement number three was on track for fun in the lightly falling snow.

Kim and Paul rode in the first sleigh and the rest fit into the remainder of the sleighs. Soft snow fell as they rode around the lake in front of them.

When the ride was completed, Kim and Paul left in his Land Rover for his home in between Evergreen and Idledale. Nancy and her mountain man left for Kim's condo and the Leawood's with their entourage left for home. What an ending to a glorious day!

Chapter Twenty-Nine

*P*aul carried Kim over the threshold of his, and now theirs, mountain home. Kim would view the house in the morning as they'd been too busy to do this before now. They'd decided that Kim needed to see all parts of the home, and then decide which one to live in and which one to sell.

After stoking a fire in the newly married couple's bedroom, Paul turned to Kim. "Finally, I get to undress my beautiful bride and show you how much I love you." Paul murmured into Kim's ear as he let out a sensuous breath next to her ear, which gave her tingles of a great and magical sort.

They fit together perfectly in a tight hug. Kim knew that Paul was the real deal as no man had ever treated her in this manner. Slowly Paul removed Kim's clothing and she helped him get his off.

Both stood naked in the light of the fire. Kim was worried as she stood naked, scars revealed and the full scoliosis of her back exposed, not sure how Paul would react to finally seeing her naked, flaws and all.

"Oh, Kim," Paul groaned aloud. "You are such a beautiful woman, truly. I love you!" He grabbed Kim's hand and drew her to him in an embrace.

"I love you, Paul." Kim whispered in his ear and Paul picked Kim up and laid her on his bed. This was their night – the first of many more to come.

They kissed with hunger, and their hands explored each other's bodies at will. Suckling on the nipples of her firm round breasts, Kim moaned with desire and pleasure as her back arched upward slightly.

Kim kissed Paul's chest through his dark hair, and she licked a few drops of the sweat beading upon his skin. She reached for the hard bulge between Paul's legs.

He groaned at her touch, and she felt a bit dominant in the moment. Kim was thrilled with the reactions she elicited from Paul. Paul was so hard, yet velvety smooth.

"Enough of that, woman. It's my turn now." With that he first stroked Kim between her legs and rang her bell. She was hot and ready for him, but Paul didn't stop.

Instead, he dove down and grasped her bell with his teeth, gently pulling and sucking until she swelled up and Kim's release sprayed him in her juices. He greedily lapped them up.

"Please, I need you now!" Kim cried out. Full of tingles and desire for Paul. He obliged by spreading her legs, settling himself between them, and sliding into her hot and ready feminine core.

Kim met each thrust Paul gave her, they were equal in their love and need for each other. Paul read only sheer joy on Kim's flushed face, no pain in her back. That drove him deeper inside her and Kim cried out when she climaxed for the second time. Paul came immediately after Kim did, and they collapsed in each other's arms, out of breath and flushed with the dewiness of sex, in total euphoria.

Kim curled up in Paul's arms and gently fell asleep after the long day she'd just had, fully sated by the rousing sex with Paul. *What a lover! Perfect! My husband! All muscle…strong…caring…her lover…her gift from God…Thank you, Lord….*

After catching soft snores from Kim, Paul soon fell asleep, content with the knowledge that she was his now and forever. Kim was his!!! Finally! *Beautiful…sexy…kind…sweet…enchanting…and in their bed…they would have many more love interludes together, now and in the future…of that he was sure….and the next interlude would happen when they woke up in the morning, on Christmas Eve…*

Nancy and her mountain man, Richard, left for Kim's condo and once there, they got comfortable in front of the fire he'd just stoked up, a glass of red wine for each.

"I've always read Kim like a book. Yet the three 'announcements' I never saw coming at all." Nancy peered at Richard, and he nodded in agreement.

"You stunned me every single time I looked at you during the gallery showing and more so, now, in the firelight. Nancy, your beauty, and kindness shine, and you have become a true mountain woman. I like everything about you right down to your heart-shaped butt. Can I ask you out on a date?" Richard implored.

Nancy blushed, then said. "I thought this was a date right now. Am I wrong?" She giggled and that set both laughing out loud.

"You can kiss me if you want to." Nancy dared him with a sweet smile. Richard swooped down and kissed Nancy like she'd never been kissed before.

They settled down and talked together, learning more about each other, and both drank a second glass of wine before Richard told Nancy goodnight at the door, and kissed her in a longing manner.

On cloud nine, Nancy fell asleep as soon as her head hit the pillow.

The Leawood's with their entourage left for home, with two very sleepy children, and happy with the wonderful day and evening spent with family and good friends. Life was marvelous.

Chapter Thirty

On Christmas morning, Kim awakened to the soft strokes of Paul's fingers in her hair, brushing it away from her face. "Good morning, Mrs. Kim Smith. How do you like being married to a doctor?" He grinned and gave her a sexy wink.

Grabbing his hand, Kim laughed and told Dr. Paul Smith to follow her. They ended up running naked into the master bath and took a slow and sensual shower. Soaping each other was erotic, and sensational. Cuddles in the shower with sweet, delicious kisses melted Kim's core and she wanted Paul more than ever.

"Slow down, Kim. I'm not done massaging soap into your back. We do have all day, after all." With that, Paul commenced a thorough sensual touch of Kim's body as she did her own of his body.

Then Kim bent over the shower railing and guided the full length of Paul into her most secret spot and sensitive area. Beyond a doubt, they both knew they would make love in the shower many times in the future.

"I love you, Kim."

"And I love you, Paul."

"When it works out right, I will take you on your dream honeymoon, I promise." Paul replied as he helped Kim dry off.

"No worries," Kim whispered into his ear. "This is our honeymoon, being with you, having your love, and me loving you back. It's Christmas time and we are together, and soon together with our extended family. We can take a vacation honeymoon any time it fits in during our lives together. You are my honeymoon, Paul."

Paul stoked the fireplace, and both fell back into the bed laughing. "I knew you were, and are, the best thing, ever, in my life, Kim. Our love will carry us through our time on planet Earth and into infinity when we become perfect souls in Heaven."

On Christmas Eve evening, everyone met up at Light of the World Catholic church for the children's mass that evening. The beautiful church with festive décor enchanted the children. Jesus' birth celebration was perfect. The final song that was sung, Silent Night, left everyone with a sense of peace.

It had been decided beforehand that everyone would then go to the Leawood home in Lakewood for the night so that they would be together come Christmas Day.

Christmas morning arrived and both Danny and Lisa were excited as they wanted to open presents under the Christmas tree.

"No presents yet." Sarah told them and she reminded both that breakfast was always first on Christmas Day.

Breakfast was buffet style, and Aaron spoke the blessing before plates were filled with bacon, sausage, eggs, hash browns, fluffy biscuits, sausage gravy, buttered toast, croissants, bagels, fresh fruit, coffee, juice, and condiments.

This year, at the table sat ten happy people who felt not only festive, but like family. Aaron sat at the head and Sarah was seated next to him. Alice sat between Danny and Lisa, Sadie found her spot next to Lisa, Kim and Paul sat next to each other, and Nancy and Richard rounded the group out.

After tucking in and eating their breakfast, everyone pitched in to help with the clean-up. Once done, the adults grabbed their coffee mugs and went to the large living room. The fire was ablaze in the fireplace and the kids smiled expectantly.

Uncle Paul acted as Santa would and withdrew wrapped packages from underneath the tree. Danny and Lisa opened their gifts first. They both had new clothing and boots along with a new bike for each, a bike to ride when the weather was nicer.

Alice received an amethyst teardrop necklace and earring set, and a gift card for her favorite bookstore.

Sadie's gift revealed a lovely tourmaline and diamond bracelet and a cash bonus from the Leawood family.

Aaron gave Sarah a nursing gift – a new handmade Imperial Royal White Faberge Egg Trinket Box of made of Vermeil GOLD and Austrian Crystal Diamonds hanging on a gold chain.

Sarah opted to give Aaron a silver, battery powered, desk clock shaped like an open suitcase containing a silver watch, stethoscope, and a physician symbol.

Paul gifted Kim with a beautiful set of Oval Emerald Solitaire Pendant with a Trio of Round Brillant Diamonds and matching earrings that looked gorgeous with Kim's green eyes.

Kim had to sneak around for Paul's gift, and when he opened his gift, he found an engraved Medical Theme Cherrywood Double Pen and Box Set along with a laser etched glass human brain model miniature – since he was a neurologist, after all.

Nancy squealed with delight when she found a gorgeous Round and Marquise Ruby Olive Branch Pendant as she loved wearing fine jewelry. She also received a lovely hand carved desk nameplate with her name to use down at the gallery.

In return, Nancy gifted Richard with a personalized wood carver tool tote bag of brown leather and inside he found a wood burner set of two pens and 15 tips.

It was truly a Christmas to remember.

Epilogue

Paul decided to sell his home and move into Kim's condo so that commuting to work was easy and Kim would have her elevator when needed.

Nancy closed on her new home December 30. Richard helped Nancy with rearranging items and most of all, their love grew with each passing day.

The new year was approaching fast, and the season was hectic, but one of pure love for all.

Biography

*M*ary L. Schmidt writes under the name of S. Jackson along with her husband, pen name A Raymond, and Mary L. Schmidt. She grew up in a small Kansas (USA) town and has lived in more than one state since then. At this time, Ms. Schmidt and her husband split their time between Kansas and Colorado (they love the mountains and off-road 4-wheeling). Traveling is one of their most favorite things to do and she always has a book or even three books to read, in the same week. Books have always been her thing. It seemed like every time she turned around, a new library card was needed due to the current one being stamped completed. Diving into a good book made any day perfect and you would be surprised at the number of books she has read over and over. She drew paper dolls and clothes for them, and with watercolor as her medium when painting scenes, especially flowers. She continued with art in high school exploring a wide variety of arts and loved it! Her creative side loves to be an amateur "shutterbug" and they have an online art gallery. In college, she went into the sciences of all things and received a bachelor's degree in the Science of Nursing. Her nursing career was highly successful, and she hung up her nursing hat in December 2012.

S. Jackson is a retired registered nurse; a member of the Catholic Church and has taught kindergarten Catechism; she has worked in various capacities for The American Cancer Society, March of Dimes, Cub, and Boy Scouts, (son, Gene, is an Eagle Scout), and sponsored trips for high school music children. She loves all forms of art but mostly focuses on the visual arts, such as amateur photography, traditional, and graphic art as her health allows.

She has written 49 books with others in various stages of production, and she is included in four anthologies.

A. Raymond is a member of the Catholic Church and has helped his wife with The American Cancer Society, March of Dimes, Cub and Boy Scouts, and sponsored children alongside his wife on music trips. He devotes his spare time to fishing, reading, playing poker, Jeeping, and traveling adventures with his wife. Spending time with their grandson, Austin, and granddaughter, Emma, happens to be another favorite past time.

Memoirs

"..point of view of a five-year-old boy ..main focus ..is to relay the love he has for his family and how grateful he was to spend every minute he could with them."

"I cried, got angry, and cheered throughout this book – it is touching, heartbreaking, difficult, powerful, and loving, all at once. Wow – what a powerful book!"
~ Monica

Visions of her Cherokee grandmother, Cordie, flashed through Mary's mind as her mother, Marguerite, informed her that her stepfathershot himself and was in the hospital. Oh no!

No! This can't be! Not after the joking around at my home last night. NO!!!!Did she use me last night? She'd never use her scapegoat child. No, she couldn't! Even Marguerite wouldn't sink that low! Or would she? Marguerite had always been abusive and vile to most people,and especially to her children and husbands, but would she shoot Harold?

Yet, here I was, and I had to tell the police that, yes, my mother was at my home all evening and into the night. How despicable that my mother connived her way into using me as her alibi. Her insanity unchecked and never stopped.

This book is a true memoir drawing upon the locals and inspiration of the areas in which the author lives and works. Names of towns, places, facilities, and people are real except for three men. Any resemblance to persons living or dead is not coincidental in nature and places where events take place are from her life growing up and as an adult.

Visions of her Cherokee grandmother, Cordie flashed through Sarah's mind as her abusive husband brutally raped her repeatedly shortly after giving birth. He took what he wanted, leaving her bloody body to be filled with years of physical pain and emotional scars that led her to believe she was worthless, and a happy life was hopeless. Sarah tried many times to leave but that was always futile. She felt useless. Her life was shattered once again when her oldest son, John, died at birth and Simon, her youngest endured a horrific cancer battle. With her only living son, Daniel she felt renewed strength knowing Cordie was watching over them always. She finally had the courage with the help of Cordie's visions from the spirit world to leave her abusive husband and make a new life for her and her son. Her new oath to her and Daniel was that no one would ever hurt either of them. Romantic love never existed for Sarah, although she had room in her heart for love. Life taught her to be wary, until the day an old friend from her past, Aaron came back into her life. Would she finally find and know true love? Could Aaron break through the walls that surrounded her? Dare she hope for love once?

Children's Books

In Davy's Dragon Castle, children learn to get along with others no matter the color of their fur or skin. It's important for children to learn the concept of, and how to not be racist and toddlers are a great age to start the teaching. Anti-racism education in elementary school starts with students' awareness of themselves, of others and of how those interactions play out. All social and emotional learning helps children to express feelings and be tuned in to the needs of others. This teaching contributes to the development of all children. Additionally, children are introduced to a character that wears a prosthetic leg, giving children a chance to learn and understand how prosthetics work and if it does/does not limit abilities. Acceptance and inclusion are important in social learning from an early age.

Tommy Turtle is a shy land turtle who likes to hide inside his shell. Tommy represents children who are shy around other children and adults, and he is nervous to play or speak. Most children are shy from time to time and it's important for children to understand shyness and how to act around others who are or aren't shy. Children need to know that shyness is normal, and they need positive encouragement from peers, family, and teachers/adults in their lives. This concept teaching can start in preschool. Children need to develop and practice social skills which will increase their quality of life in school through drama class, music, gym class, show and tell time, play time and more, rather than staying on the sidelines and simply watching others and having less friends and social isolation. If confidence is learned, self-esteem increases, and children succeed. Less confidence promotes increased shyness. It is essential to praise children for their successes and not shame them at all when they fail. All social and emotional learning helps children to express feelings and be tuned in to the needs of others.

"Love the parent
and educator guide
in the back. Teach
your child good
touch/bad touch,
and body ownership!"

"Take a stand today
and build up your
child's self-esteem!
Stop bullies and
child suicide!"

Available at Amazon, Walmart, and All Bookstores!